Choices

A Collection of
Questionable
Decisions

A Temptation Press Anthology

Choices

A Collection of Questionable Decisions

A Temptation Press Anthology

TEMPTATION PRESS

This book is a work of fiction. Any references to historical events, real people, or real locales are used fictitiously. All characters appearing in this work are the product of the individual author's imagination, and any resemblance to actual persons, living or dead is entirely coincidental.

Trade Paper ISBN: 978-1-947210-28-8
Kindle ISBN: 978-1-947210-29-5
Digital ISBN: 978-1-947210-30-1
Library of Congress Control Number: 2018902378

First Edition: March 2018
10 9 8 7 6 5 4 3 2 1

Acknowledgements

Temptation Press would like to thank all those that contributed to this anthology. We chose to showcase six new voices that best represented our vision for this work.

We would also like to thank our Temptation Press team for all their dedication and hard work to these projects.

Contents

Willingly Trapped

Pamela Brodman

Chapter I

"Can you stay the night at least?" I asked him, hoping that for once he would do something I wanted him to do. Without even pausing in putting his clothes back on, he glanced over his heavily tattooed shoulder and shook his head.

"Nah, can't. She'll be getting in early in the morning, and she hasn't given me an estimate. So I don't wanna risk the chance of not being there," he said. He finally turned to me as he buttoned up his blue striped shirt, giving me the intense urge to rip it off him.

I looked up into his light-blue eyes, not liking the disinterest I found there. Not a look a woman wants to see on the man she just had sex with, really. More and more I was starting to hate the little arrangement we had.

"Tell me again why I continue to do this?" I asked, anger quickly making me forget the last two and a half hours we had spent in bed.

"Don't start with this, Ella. I really don't have time. I want to get some shut-eye before she arrives," he replied impatiently as he tied his black dress shoes, but he quickly flashed me one of his wicked grins and added, "You've worn me out, baby."

"Told you to not call me baby," I whispered as he disappeared into the bathroom. Louder, wanting to have him hear me over the running water as he brushed his teeth, I said, "This is the last time."

One second, two seconds, and the running water stopped. He stepped into view. "What?"

I swallowed, and repeated, "I said that this is the last time. After tonight, no more."

He strode all the way into the bedroom. I sat up in the large bed, holding the blanket up to cover my breasts. Quite ridiculous, seeing how he has had three months of clear viewing. Still, it was automatic. Like bringing up a shield. With him, I was going to need it.

"Do you really believe that?" he asked as he leaned forward on the bed bracing himself on his arms. For a moment my gaze fell to his lips. He was close enough to kiss, and my stomach turned with the mere thought of it. Still, I brought my eyes up to his and nodded.

He chuckled, gave me a quick peck, then retreated back into the bathroom. I sat there wondering if I finally had freed myself, but his deep voice came to tear me from that thought.

"Baby, you know as well as I that you'll be asking me back into your bed next weekend after work."

The arrogant bastard, I thought. *When did it happen that I let him be that sure of me?* A one-night stand had turned into a three-month affair; not being a girlfriend, not being exclusive. He was a man that couldn't be tied down, he repeated over and over. He offered me amazing sex and some degree of companionship, but beyond that, we were free to do as we wished. Sadly for me and my twisted sense of loyalty, I couldn't possibly sleep with or date anyone other than him. Which left me with nights spent wondering if he was in another woman's bed. Never would have believed myself the jealous type, but on those nights, I couldn't deny it.

"No. We are done with this little game," I snapped back, surprising myself at the steady, angry tone I used. When he came out of the bathroom this time, he looked pissed off. I couldn't help but cower.

"I thought we were clear on this from the beginning. So, what is the problem now?" he asked, or rather growled. He leaned on the door frame, arms crossing over his chest, and legs crossing at the ankles. He was the very picture of annoyance.

"You are the problem. Your arrogance is frankly a turn-off," I bravely said. *Where did I get the courage to say this to him?* I could see my reflection in the mirror behind him. I didn't look particularly courageous, with a mess of curls about my face and brown eyes slightly smeared with the evening eye-makeup. I definitely looked like I had a long rump between the sheets.

"Is it?" he asked. I didn't like the purposeful look he gave me. As if he knew precisely just how much I wanted him back in bed. "I don't think that is it at all. My arrogance isn't the issue here," he paused. "The other women are."

I couldn't keep my face from showing he had hit the mark. My secret was out. *Now what? He'll simply walk off and bid me farewell, right? Exactly what I wanted, no?* It was what all my friends had been advising, to end it. My silence didn't do much to disprove his deduction.

He remained in the same spot, his face unreadable. "You could have just asked me to stop seeing other women."

"Would you have?" I asked with some doubt.

"No," he shrugged. "But I would have lied about it."

I couldn't help but laugh at that. I bitter laugh, mind you. I was not at all amused by his callousness. "Leave."

"Now, now, baby," he cooed as he pushed himself off the door frame and came towards the bed, the wicked grin back on his lips and eyes pleading. "We can figure this out without going for the extreme, can't we?"

"Leave," I said again, though this time I lost the conviction to back up the order. He kept coming, unbuttoning his shirt and leaving it hanging open to act as a frame for the perfect picture of his broad chest and mouth-watering abs. I didn't move when his hands found my ankles between the rumpled blanket and sheets.

"You really don't want me to leave, and I really don't feel like going. Not just yet," he said and gave one hard tug of my ankles, making me slide on the bed toward him.

Damn him! I still held on to the corner of the blanket covering me, not willing to make the conquest easier on him.

I glared at him, wanting so badly to tell him to go to hell. Instead, all that escaped me was a moan as his hands wandered up my legs and disappeared under the bunched-up blanket.

Chapter II

Next morning, I braced myself for the tongue lashing I was sure to get from Sabina. "Ella, you aren't seriously considering staying with him after last night, are you?" she challenged angrily. I couldn't help but look away from my best friend. "Tell me you aren't!?"

"What would you have me do? I am unhappy about it, but not having him in my life would make me downright miserable!" I hissed back, conscious of the other people dining around us. The booth was by far not private enough to have this sort of conversation. It was obvious that Sabina had no such worries as she glared at me with her accusing hazel eyes.

"But he is such an asshole! Good sex does not make up for the treatment he is giving you," she said, pausing long enough on her tirade to take a sip of her cider. The pizza sat cooling in the middle of the table, yet untouched. "Besides, knowing you, you don't even see that other men would treat you like a queen if you stopped this affair with him."

"I still go out and party!" I tried to defend myself, though it seemed rather futile since I knew how right she was.

"Yeah, and at the end of the night you go home alone, or wait for him to text you and ask you to come over."

I took a slice of pizza and laid it on my plate, trying to give me some time to respond to that. Nothing came to mind as I burned my tongue on the first bite. "Damn!" I mumbled as I huffed and puffed.

"I still think you should give him the door next time," she added while tucking her short brown hair behind her ear so she could take a bite of pizza.

I grimaced, but coolly I was quick to point out, "So says the woman with a devoted husband."

"Hey, well, you could get the same thing if you let this idiot go," she said waving her hand absently.

"Is not like I can say he's cheating. We never said that we were exclusive to one another," I sighed, "which he is quick to mention often enough."

Sabina's long, hard stare didn't improve my mood. I took a drink of the cider and tried to change the conversation. "So, are we going out tonight?"

"I don't know. I didn't hear back from the other two, and I haven't even asked my husband. He knows just how crazy we get when we go out, and he's probably not going to be happy about him not going."

"Isn't that the point of a Girls' Night Out? No men?" I laughed. I could just imagine why exactly her husband would like to be around. How a socialite like her ended up with a recluse like him was pretty incredible.

A melodic ring came from my purse sitting beside me on the booth bench. She frowned and I stared at the offending purse. Before I reached for the phone, I knew who it was. Apparently, so did she. I watched her as she got out of the booth and headed for the ladies' room, long legs carrying her gracefully across the restaurant's floor in an enviable way.

"Hello?"

"Where are you, beautiful?" Came the voice on the other end. I was smiling before I could help myself.

"Having lunch with a friend," I said trying to sound curt. Don't think he bought it hearing him chuckle.

"I can just imagine who you are with. Say 'hi' to her from me," he teased, knowing well enough how much she disliked him. "How long are you going to be?"

I glanced back to see if she was coming back, "We just got the food, so it will be another hour probably."

"I will be at your place in an hour and a half, then," he said, and I couldn't help but hold my breath.

Finally, I said, "I am going out with the girls tonight."

"That's cool, we still have enough time. I am meeting some business partners later, but wanted to see you before I went."

"You mean you wanted to have sex before you went," I was able to say. There was silence at the other end of the line. When his voice broke it, I was startled.

"Why are you making it complicated, Ella? We have a good thing going,"

I laughed at that, "For you, it is!"

"I don't hear you complain—"

"Oh, don't even say it!" I interrupted him. Sabina returned at that moment, giving me a surprised look. I must have been louder than I intended. "Look, I can't see you today. I am sure you'll be able to find another one tonight."

She almost clapped at that.

"Fine. Whatever you want," he said to my utter shock. Next thing I knew, the line went dead.

Chapter III

Blinking once, then twice, I still couldn't believe what I was seeing. His car sat idling in my driveway. Not something I expected to see after returning from the restaurant.

"What are you doing here?" I asked him when he came out of the car, suit perfectly pressed and his grin ready for me.

"I wanted to see you, so I came over," he said like that was the most obvious thing. "I've been waiting for half an hour. I almost thought you were standing me up."

"You can hardly say I stood you up if I did not make plans with you," I said testily. I made it to my front door, realizing he was following me. "I am not inviting you in."

"Why are you angry with me? I never played games with you." This brought me up short. I turned to look at him, key in hand. "You know I never lied to you, I was straight up about what we were both going to get out of this."

Grinding my teeth, I opened the door, paused and exhaled. "So sex is all you want, right?"

He looked as if I wounded him deeply, and with something close to a pout he answered, "Don't put it like that. I enjoy your company, baby."

"Do you?"

"Yes, of course, I do!" he insisted.

"Then explain why you refused every invitation to go out? Why you could never meet me unless it was your place or mine?" I challenged, crossing my arms and in doing so, successfully blocking the door so that he stood out on the porch. I wanted my answer, damn it!

For a long minute, there was nothing. He looked uncomfortable and unsure. I couldn't help but enjoy it.

It was short lived though.

Stepping up right under the threshold, within inches of where I was, his hand went to my nape. The familiar thrill, followed by the delicious warmth spreading quickly all the way to my toes, my stomach doing its usual butterfly dance … this man knew how my body responded to his.

Entirely too well.

I held my place for a heartbeat, then I could not keep my lips from parting, awaiting his kiss.

"I dislike sharing your attention," he murmured right before he took that last step that brought him all the way into the house, pushing me right along with him. He had the afterthought of shutting the door behind him as we tumbled to the floor. His hands easily maneuvered himself to find me wet and willing. With a hard cry, he pushed himself inside me, so rough that my tailbone dug into the carpet.

Automatically my legs wrapped around his hips, wanting him to thrust even deeper. His teeth sank into my breast's tender flesh. The pain was muted against the buildup to my climax, and I surrendered myself to it. My legs went limp as he pumped once, twice, and finally, his own orgasm hit him. His growl and shudder were like a badge of honor that I could bring him to such pleasure.

He stood smoothly, bringing me up with him. In a daze, I let him guide me. I woke hours later, thankfully tucked in my bed with him next to me. My cell was ringing. Without a doubt, it was one of the girls wondering what the hell had happened to me. I considered letting it ring until the voicemail picked up, but my guilt won out.

"What the fuck? Where the hell are you?" screamed a familiar voice, and from the boisterous noise going on in the background, Sabina was already at the bar. I winced at the angry tone of her voice. I guess it was a really bad thing to ditch your best friend.

"Look, tell the others I am sorry, but I won't make it out tonight. Something came up," I whispered trying not to wake him.

I could almost see her taking a deep breath to calm herself, and then the loudness of the bar almost banished. She had stepped outside, "Yeah, I see. He's there."

"I will talk to you tomorrow, okay? I'm really, really sorry, Sabina," I tried again.

"Fine, but I really don't want to hear any more about this shit, Ella. He is a dick and fucked up for doing what he is doing to you," she said with all her anger behind it. "But whatever, what would I know. Have a great night."

"You too," I began, but she had already hung up. *Shit*, this was really starting to mess me up.

I put the phone back on the nightstand and turned over to find him staring at me. "You think I am an asshole now, don't you?"

"I never doubted it," I told him without pause. He raised his head from the pillow, propping it on his arm and he chuckled. *Did it always have to be a battle of witty or sardonic comments?* I couldn't remember when we ever had a normal conversation with the sole purpose of finding out more about one another. I guess that should have been one of the big hints that this was never going to reach anything above a 'fuckbuddy' relationship. Despite any hope I might have for the contrary.

"Didn't you have a meeting with some partners from work?"

"Nah, I rescheduled," he said, his hand lazily tracing my naked navel and hip. It was a distraction, but I wasn't ready to make him stop. "I had something more important to tend to."

"What was that?" I asked, half fearing his answer.

"A beautiful woman who was unhappy with me."

"Was?" I couldn't stop from raising an eyebrow at that.

His hand dipped lower, and he kissed me on the shoulder, "I am certain I have made a very good attempt at making her happy once more."

I had a witty retort for that. I honestly did, but he was quick to make me forget all about talking or at least, anything that would make any sense.

When I next checked my cell, late the following afternoon, I had missed three calls and gotten five text messages. My best friend had the patience of a saint for putting up with me and all this drama.

Chapter IV

A month later, I clutched my cellphone as if I could just strangle him through it. "I'm such a gullible idiot!" I screamed at the fogged-up mirror in the bathroom. I wished I had the kind of temperament to throw or break things when angered. It would have helped immensely, but unfortunately, I was too much of a neat freak.

"Fool!" I hissed at my mirror image. I had stepped out of the shower to find a missed call from him, followed by a text message. He would not be visiting me this evening after all. He had decided to drive two hours to visit some friends out of town and would most likely stay there until the weekend. *Why am I surprised? Not like he hadn't done this in the past.* Dinner plans, movie plans ... nothing was good enough to keep him from breaking them. Especially if he had to be in my company. I angrily stormed into my bedroom and came to a decision. For weeks

I had been marinating and agonizing over this, but I had just been pushed to the brink.

"Yeah, what's up?" Sabina answered after just two rings.

"I'm taking it." Not missing a beat, I heard her long sigh. "I know this is the only way I will have to get away from him. I'm not strong enough to simply turn him away. I have fallen in love with the bastard, can you believe it?"

There was no surprise in her voice when she replied. "Honey, you were in love with him long before he came between your thighs for the first time. You were simply too stubborn to admit it. Your passion will be the end of you if it's given to men like him."

"Well, aren't you the wise old crone this evening," I said dryly.

"I've been reading 'An idiot's guide to being a wise philosopher' and thought to share my enlightenment," she laughed. "Will you tell him, or simply leave?"

"I doubt he would miss me at all. More and more he keeps going out of town lately. I do believe he's found a replacement for me already."

Silence from the other end. "If I were smarter I wouldn't ask this, but I've already proven my idiocy time and time again," I say, feeling my stomach begin to sink, my insides tightening into awful, painful knots. "You know something, don't you?"

"Will it change your mind about taking the job?" she asked instead. It gave me my answer. He had met someone, and I was no longer in the picture. The fact he kept the little bit of contact with me was simply to save face. Soon I would be getting the friendship speech.

"I'm going. He had been the only thing that kept me here since you moved. Now he is the reason why I must get away. Ironic, isn't it?" My humor was quick in its death, and I could hardly swallow the lump in my throat. I looked up at my rather bland white ceiling to keep the tears from spilling over.

"Oh, sweetie! Don't do that, he doesn't deserve tears from you. He deserves nothing from you, you hear?"

"Yeah. I know. Listen, I'm going down to the bar to have a drink. I can't stay in." I said quickly. At least I wasn't sobbing.

Another pause and I knew I had worried her. "Are you sure you want to do that? I wish I still lived near you."

"No, you don't, you love it there, and you know it. But I miss you, too. I'll be alright. Just need something to keep my mind off of this for the night. I'll call you tomorrow."

Another two hours and I was firmly planted on a stool at the nearly empty local Irish pub, a strong Old Fashioned at hand, chatting with my Reese, my bartender friend. I was there for less than an hour and two drinks into it when in walked the rowdiest bunch that could be found on a Tuesday night.

"Really? I so don't need this tonight," I mumbled as the large group of men came storming into the bar, singing at the top of their lungs, arms drunkenly about one another's shoulders. I shared a bemused look with the bartender and watched the men spread out over the two booths directly behind me. One of them dislodged himself from the group and approached the bar. Wide smile, laughing green eyes and about six feet of tanned muscle. I could scarcely keep from staring.

He noticed and stared back as he leaned on the bar very close to me and yelled at the bartender, "Oy! Beer. Lots of it! Keep 'em coming, too."

I'll be damned! It would seem I had just found myself amidst a hoard of Aussies. As he turned to face me, I couldn't help but smile. Freckles covered his face from cheek to cheek, giving him an almost childlike innocence that belied his extremely masculine character.

"Alo, there! You drinking alone, or should I be worrying about some bloke coming any second?" He asked outright. He even looked over his shoulder toward the front door and then toward the bathroom.

I had to laugh, he looked genuinely scared. "No company tonight. Just me," I answered, the ice clinking in my nearly empty glass.

"Now, that's a terrible thing! No Sheila ought to be drinking alone," and without further ado, he lifted me off my stool, and to my mortification, and much to the delight of his mates, brought me to their table.

"Listen up, you rotten lot! This here Sheila is gonna sit and drink with us. Let's not lair it up and frighten her away, clear?" He yelled at them as he sat me down. I introduced myself to them, trying hard to keep up with all the new names being thrown at me in between the barely understood compliments.

"Don't mind them, darling. One would think they've never seen a beauty before," he whispered in my ear. I could hardly mind having all this male attention. One didn't get that often.

The hours and the drinks passed by and I liked this green-eyed sweetheart more and more.

"Why were you alone tonight, darling?" He suddenly asked. His seriousness caught me off guard, and I answered without thinking.

"I came to get my mind used to the idea of moving away from here and its sordid memories."

"Ah, were these sordid memories attached to a man, then?"

"Isn't that usually the case?"

"Indeed, it is." I respected the fact he didn't give me a pitying look. Instead, "Nothing a drink and good company can't make you forget," he said.

I felt the giddiness of a buzz kicking in.

"And where is this job you are taking going to place you?"

"Two years in our sister company in England."

He looked pensive, then looked me straight in the eye and asked me, "Does your company work out of Australia as well?"

"I think so. It's a large enough company, but I've never really asked." The bar was closing, and his buddies were none-too steadily filing out of the place. I forgot all about his question.

"Shouldn't you be going with them?"

"I have you to take home first. I'll meet up with them at the hotel. They're drunk, but I don't have to worry about them." He looked down at me and smiled, "You, I wouldn't leave you out of my sight for a moment."

"Aren't you chivalrous?" I jabbed him in his ribs as we headed towards my car.

"And you are very charming, Ella," he said and tucked my arm under his. Then I almost missed a step when he asked, "Any chance I could see you again tomorrow? Lunch maybe?"

Woah! Was I heading in this direction again so quickly? Not mere hours ago I was feeling heartbroken over that asshole. But here I am now, considering a date with a virtual stranger. *Did I need a man this badly in my life?*

Noting my hesitation, he went on. "I know I'm only here through the week, but I would like very much to see you again and you really ought to give a block a fair go."

Looking at him, I couldn't see any reason why I couldn't meet him again. Why I shouldn't just take him for who he appeared to be and see where it would take me. Didn't I earn that? "I would enjoy seeing you again, too." As soon as the breathless words left my mouth, he leaned in and kissed me hard and deep. There was no shyness here. The force of his passion matched my own, and I found my hands rising on their own accord and burying themselves in his thick brown hair. He pulled me closer until our bodies were flushed against each other. Damn, but it had been a long time since I had kissed someone different. I had forgotten the thrill of a first kiss and the consuming heat from a man's passionate embrace when he is desperate to have you.

"I will drive you home and take a cab to the hotel, will that be alright?"

"Yes, of course."

I handed him my keys, and we drove the twenty minutes to my place holding hands over the gear shift, our fingers interlacing, and at every red light he would lean over and kiss me. Sometimes sweetly and slowly tracing his tongue over my bottom lip, or catching it gently between his teeth. But sometimes it was with such hunger that my lips would feel raw and swollen afterward. By the time he pulled up to my driveway, I had no intention of letting him catch that cab back to his hotel.

I pulled him inside and somehow managed to reach the bedroom, stumbling over ourselves as we peeled off each layer of clothing. Naked, we fell onto the bed, a tangle of legs and arms. His kisses grew deeper, longer. He held my face between his hands, trapping it there to better access every recess of my mouth. Having him beneath me, allowed my hands to roam freely over his wide shoulders and thickly corded back. Freckles dusted the skin over his chest and shoulders, and I traced my hands over them as if trying to connect the dots and draw something. My roving fingers traced lower and lower, over abs that I could count, following the thin trail of tightly coiled hair to the end. When I enveloped him in my hand, he gasped and pulled back from our heated kiss. *Oh, yes! I have definitely earned this.*

"Ah, Ella, you are going to be the death of me tonight with those hands of yours," he whispered against my mouth.

I laughed softly, "Wait until you feel what I can do with my mouth, then."

He threw his head back and moaned as I slid down his body. But I didn't get far before he stopped me and flipped me on my back and pinned me down with his solid weight.

"Oh, no, darling," he says teasingly. "Ladies cum first."

Not one to put up an argument with a gentleman, I closed my eyes and allowed my senses to drown in sensual delight.

Chapter V

I came awake the next morning to find hooded green eyes gazing sleepily at me. I stretched lazily, and his large hand splayed possessively over the curve of my hip. *I could definitely get used to this.*

"G'dye, dahlin'," he said with a thicker accent than I had heard from him so far. Sleep apparently made his tongue a bit lazy. I smiled and was rewarded with a sweet peck on the lips.

"Good morning. Hope your friends aren't worried that I kidnaped you."

He sighed dramatically, and with a pained look, he said, "I'll have to report how you attacked me and took advantage of my helpless body. They'll never let me live it down."

"Well, you should never trust an American woman. We are quite the vicious lot." I rolled out of bed and headed for the shower. "You can nap a little longer … or you can join me in the shower. Gentleman's choice."

"How about you let me make you breakfast," he said. *Well, so the man had talents that extended beyond the bedroom?* This I was also eager to enjoy.

I felt glorious and surprisingly happy. Happier than I have been in months, it seemed. Could a good one-night stand do this much for a heartbroken girl? It would seem so. I wrapped myself in a towel and with my hair still dripping wet I left the confines of the bedroom in pursuit of the delicious smells coming from my kitchen. What I found instead made my knees buckle under me, falling with a thud on the soft carpet.

The Aussie was the first to reach me on the floor, garbed still in only his boxer briefs. Not two feet from where he had been, in a perfectly pressed business suit, stood the man I had gone to the bar to drink away. He was angry. But hell, I was pissed!

"Are you alright, darling?"

"Yeah, why is he here?" I realized who I was mistakenly asking, and I faced the guilty one, "What are you doing here?"

"Obviously intruding," he said, sparing a glance to the Aussie. "I came because I heard about that job offer you took. Apparently, I was to hear it from colleagues first, instead of you."

"Sorry, Ella. I shouldn't have let him in," Green Eyes whispered as he helped me up.

"No, I'm alright. Thank you," I assured him.

I saw the small banquet he had prepared for us, and I realized how screwed up my life had been, that the man preparing me breakfast for the first time was someone I just met the night before. I had fallen for the wrong man indeed.

"Leave my house. I'm taking the job. We will be free of each other from now on. We both will be much happier this way." I said, staring him right in the eyes. He tugged at the tie in his collar and ran a frustrated hand through his short hair.

"That's it? You fuck the first guy you pick up in a bar, and suddenly the months we were together are out the window? That's a bit cold, don't you think?" He asked staring now at the man in question.

I felt him tense next to me, and I stepped in between the two of them. I had intended to break the line of sight, but I realized that I was much shorter than the two of them and they could easily continue their eye contest over my head. I was not about to have a brawl in my own home, damn it!

"How dare you!?" *The nerve of him,* I thought. "You have no qualms about making it clear to me that you are fucking other women, but when I … you know what?" I shook my head and pointed at the door. I must say that having to grip my towel to keep it from falling ruined the 'Strong, Mature Woman' image I was striving for. "Get the hell out of my home. Don't make me tell you again."

He came towards me, eyes hard and mouth drawn to a thin line.

I unconsciously stepped back, right into the new and seemingly protective man in my life. His hands came to rest on my still damp shoulders. "I think she was pretty clear, mate. Shove off!"

"Shut the hell up! This is between her and me," he said coldly.

"Well, I really think I just got involved."

With that instigation, old lover boy fisted his hands and stepped closer still. "You will be if you don't move aside."

"Is that a threat?" The Aussie asked, his grip on my shoulders getting tighter as he got angrier.

"Are you deaf now, too? I said get the hell out of here!"

"It isn't for you to order me out. And I believe she asked you to leave first." *Well, wasn't the Aussie getting smug?*

How the hell did this come about? I just wanted to savor my one-night stand, breakfast included, without the drama that had been following me since I set myself up as this man's lover. Now the drama was developing into a full out soap opera, right in my living room!

"No, no, no," I yelled at them both. That caught their attention. I shrugged out of the Aussie's tight hold and stepped up to what had suddenly become a testosterone contest. "You will not start this shit in my house. Both of you, out of here this instant!"

In unison, they argued this decision. Neither clearly wanting to leave, both astonished I had asked them to. Silently I marched into the bedroom, gathered up whatever stuff the Aussie had sprawled on my floor, as well as any items Mr. Wrong had left in my place during our whatever-hell-of-a-relationship-you-wanna-call-it, and stormed back out making a beeline for the front door. I smirked as both followed me, just like puppies wanting their toys.

"Darling, what are you doing?" The Aussie asked. I was not going to state the obvious. He will see for himself once I threw all their crap on my front lawn for them to pick up. Right after my door was firmly locked behind them, of course.

"You don't want to do this. You know I want you in my life, and that I care a lot about you." Those words that had made me melt after any fight with him in the past, sounded so empty and hollow now, meaningless words meant to manipulate and avoid further confrontation. *A fool with her heart on a sleeve, that's what I had been.*

"Fetch now, boys!" I said as I strew my armload across the dewy grass. I was mildly surprised that the Aussie wasn't the first to dive for his stuff. He gave me one long look that could have said a thousand things, but none would have been anger. Damn, but I did regret not meeting him during different circumstances. But I shook my head, and with a sad smile and a wink, he followed the other one onto the lawn.

Calmly I walked back inside, closed the door and threw the bolt.

Breakfast was waiting.

What Love Has Taught Me

Malorie Mackey

Looking back on my life, I realize that I've never been normal, and I see now how extraordinary that is. My husband found my journal from when I was thirteen years old, and I let him read it. He encouraged me to put this out there as it is very open, very true, and something I think everyone who is finding themselves should read.

As my husband handed me my journal from that time, I nervously opened it to re-read it. My hands were shaking as I opened to a story I knew well. A story of self-discovery. I was afraid to re-live the excitement and heartbreak of it again, as I knew all too well how it was going to end.

You see, in the pages of this journal is where I wrote about being confused and afraid until I finally accepted myself and became confident in my relationship with a girl. The girl, however, Angela, never really got too comfortable being with me. At the time, she couldn't accept how society might see her. But who can blame her? We were so young.

Here's our story. Though it doesn't necessarily end happily for us together, it helped shape who I am as a person, and it helped me grow comfortable with myself. I know it did the same for Sara, too.

As I began to read my old story, I appreciated what it had to offer, so I trudged through and read the first excerpt I found about my confusion. Who was I? Clearly, I was unsure. It seemed like the usual story of a teen trying to find herself, but then it progressed from there. It was clear, originally, that I was too afraid to confess to myself that I had feelings for a girl, so the entries were very masked. But they quickly became more and more open.

2/25/02

Where do I go from here? That's what I ask myself sometimes. I am: Lost; A Christian; Confused; A Teen. I don't like life at times.

2/27/02

I am so confused. I can't stand my step-dad. I want to live with my dad, but I don't want to hurt my mom or my step-dad's feelings. I love and believe in God and am devoted to him, but I am also very confused about myself and my feelings.

To my mom—I've always been a momma's girl, but we've separated a lot lately, and it's because of David. I can't tell you a lot about myself now. I will be a problem for you. I would be in trouble, but the rules have changed, and I'm a teenager. Though I still love you, I find it hard to think that you will understand me when you find out the feelings that I've been having.

3/23/02

I am confused once again. I'll start with this: Sara and I got into a discussion today about how we would react if we had a friend who was gay or if a friend were in love with us. Or if that were you, how could you tell them?

I'm just going to open up and be less cryptic. I discovered two weeks ago that I wasn't sure about my sexual identity. It's horrible—not to know at all. I think I could be falling in love for the first time in my life but with my best friend ... a girl. And it's scary. I even think she feels the same way. The way we act around each other is so touchy; it's indescribable. What's happening to me? What's going on? That's all I can really say right now. I guess it's silly. I'll probably look back on this and laugh or make fun of myself, but I do know one thing: no matter what, right now, Sara is my best friend, and that will never change. My heart wouldn't let it.

3/25/02

I'm never understood. My mom occasionally does understand me, but David NEVER could. I have to love him, but sometimes I hate that. As far as Sara, what is life without love? I'll tell you. It's a lonely mess. And life with love is confusing.

Do I really love Sara? Who knows.

4/8/02

Okay, I really do love God, and I am a Christian. I've heard from my mother and stepfather that you go to

Hell if you are gay, but I really don't think that's true. I really might be in love with Sara, and I can't help it. I don't want to betray God, but she kissed me on the head today, and I melted. But why would God create us this way if it were wrong? It doesn't feel wrong, and I can't imagine it being so.

4/10/02

I think it's true. I think Sara likes me. She hugged me for a full minute in the hall, and we were holding hands during play practice. She grabbed my hand, told me it felt right and kissed me on the cheek.

4/13/02

Sara and I went to a dance last night. As our friends were dancing with boys, we sat out. She looked at me and told me that it would be better to date a girl than a boy because girls understand each other better. She went on about how she'd prefer to date girls. I agreed and laughed. Then, the last dance of the night, the 5th slow dance (as I recall), Sara and I slow danced together. I think I really love her. I don't know if we are considering going out or taking it further, but I know that dancing with her felt right.

4/20/02

Love

A noun.

1.   A strong attachment, affection, or devotion for a person or persons

2.   A strong liking for or interest in something

3.   *A strong, passionate affection for someone of the opposite sex*

These are the top three definitions of love in the dictionary today.

My thoughts on love now that I'm sure I've experienced it:

I agree with the first definition which states that love is a strong attachment, affection, or devotion to a person. I don't agree at all with the third definition. It couldn't only be for someone of the opposite sex. What about gay people? They are people, too.

Therefore, this is my definition of love: Love is when you long to be around someone and care for their every thought and move. You always want to be near them and hold them. You feel drawn to them and wish to be a bigger part of their life.

After analyzing the dictionary, which might be a bit obsessive, I have concluded that I love Sara.

4/24/02

I was feeling terribly depressed after our school production of "Annie" ended. I can't see Sara every day now. I gave her a note, defeated, feeling as if I have nothing else to live for. Her response:

"Always remember how much I love you. I'd do anything to make you feel better. We're friends always. The world is a great place."

I am rather frightened. I realize that Sara is the first girl that I've ever loved. The first person, none the less. I have a family, but that's not this feeling of love. Sure, there's friend love, but that can't compare. How I feel *about Sara isn't comparable to anything. This is real. I long to be around her. Sure, I've gone out with a boy or had a crush, but not like this. This is an indescribable feeling.*

4/25/02

As I sit here at the campground around the invisible fire, two scenes float in and out of my head.

Scene 1- Sara puts down her note and looks at me; she looks nervous and quickly says, "I don't know." With that, she sticks out her hand across the table to me, and I put my hand in hers, "Best friends forever no matter what."

"Of course. Do you hate me?"

"Of course not." She paused, "Let's talk about it later."

Scene 2- I began talking to Sara about how I danced with Damian that morning at a Spanish assembly. She looked hurt, "That's good. You like him, but you went back on our word that boys are evil."

"No Sara. I didn't. It wasn't my choice, and I don't know if I like him anymore."

"Then who do you like?"

"No one."

"Me?" She glared at me.

I replied, "Of course."

She followed up, "As what?"

"I don't know."

"Me either. Are we really ... gay?"

We were silent for a second before she added, "Well if I'm gay then there's two strikes against me in life."

"Strikes?"

"Things that make people not like me."

I followed, "Anyone who really is your friend will always like you no matter who you are as a person."

With that, lunch ended.

How do those two scenes fit together? Well, scene 2 happened yesterday at lunch. That made me think that she really was falling in love with me, too. That night, I wrote her a note, continuing our discussion. It stated that I had fallen in love with her and asked if she wanted to go out with me. Then it explained that what she claimed were "strikes" against her were not. I asked her not to hate me and the bottom. In the morning, I gave it to her. Then scene 1 went into effect.

We're going to talk about everything on Sunday night over the phone. I'm so nervous. Perhaps socially she is too afraid to do something this unheard of. People don't look fondly of girls dating girls here in Virginia. She does seem to be very concerned about what people will think of her.

Well, I hope she likes me. She said she didn't hate me and that we'll always be friends. Since I'm camping, I wanted to get that off my chest so I can enjoy this event now.

5/1/02

I am the happiest girl in the world right now! Sara and I were writing notes back and forth in our notebook (which I'll post below), and, long story short, we are going out. She is officially my girlfriend! Plus, after lunch, she asked me to be her date to the 8th-grade dance. And I am so elated. See our correspondence in the notebook right here below.

From The Notebook:

Sara: Hey Mal, so we definitely need to talk. Are we going to stay best friends or… be more than that? It's up to you. I'll be happy either way, but if we do choose to be together, we have to keep it a secret. Love, Sara

Me: Dear Sara, Obviously, I would love it if we would try to be together, and I am fine keeping it a secret. If you'd have me as your girlfriend, that would be great. But, if not, that's okay with me. Love, Malorie

Sara: Well, the final vote is in. Let's try it. We don't have to take it fast, but I do think I'm in love with you. But if it ever feels wrong, tell me, and we can stop. Love, Sara

Me: I really am the happiest girl in the world right now. I have been falling in love with you, and I'm happy you feel the same way.

Sara: What more is there to say?

Me: Well Sara, I'm so excited about the 8th-grade dance. It is going to be so fun. And what you said to me before, it will never feel weird to me because it's love. And love never feels wrong."

5/2/02

At this point, I am mindless. I am a young person in love. That's all I can say. Today at lunch, Lacie asked,

"If one of my friends wanted to go out with you, would you say yes?"

I replied, "I know you're talking about Damian. Tell him that I'm sorry, but we can't go out.

Sara grabbed my hand under the lunch table. "She's already taken."

Lacie, "By Who?"

I looked concerned as Sara had told me that we should protect ourselves and not tell anyone ... "Uh ... a boy from my old school ..."

Later, at the end of lunch, we went in the bathroom. After everyone left but us, we hugged for about a minute straight before someone came in, and we leapt away from each other. We were laughing uncontrollably when we made it back over to the lunch table.

Lacie asked, "I don't want to know, do I?"

"You really don't," Sara said between giggles.

5/5/02

Today at lunch, I was sitting with Lacie, Alicia, and Sara. Lacie exclaimed, "Malorie, you and Alicia are so lucky because you're the only two of us with boyfriends! I'm jealous."

Sara looked at me with the most hurt expression and exclaimed, "You do?"

She is terrible at keeping this discrete, which is what she wanted. Personally, I don't care who knows- except my family right now. My mom wouldn't understand.

I turned back over to her and said, with a heavy undertone, "Yes, I do. Remember?"

"Oh yeah, of course." She laughed it off.

Anyway, then I went to church with my parents and came back. This is what I've decided: Just because I'm gay doesn't mean that my relationship with God will change. How can love be a sin? I'm sure it isn't. And as far as my sins, he will always forgive me for them and love me as I am.

5/6/02

A continuation of our notebook conversation from Sara to myself and back again:

Malorie: Hey Sara, since you are my date to the 8th-grade dance, would you like to slow dance? If so, should we find a spot where there aren't going to be a lot of people or just dance in front of everyone else? I really don't care which. It doesn't bother me if people see us. Love, a very bored Malorie.

P.S. If you wanted to kiss me, I wouldn't oppose. I am happy and comfortable with you as long as you are happy and comfortable with me.

Sara: Mal, I would be honored if you wanted to slow dance with me. And I would like to kiss you. It makes me nervous, you know, but I want to. Sorry I suck at writing notes, as you can tell.

Malorie: Sara, Yay! Slow dancing would be great. And, yes, I feel nervous about kissing you, too, but I'm sure it will be great. I love you. And you're notes aren't terrible. They are comforting to me.

Sara: Have you ever kissed anyone, like a real kiss, before? Also, I know boys keep asking you out. If they ask you to dance at the event, you should do it. That way people don't know. But if they ask you out, I will hunt them down.

Malorie: I have kissed someone once, but it was on the cheek. It didn't mean anything. It was my old boyfriend at my old middle school. I won't dance with any guys, don't worry. Even if they ask. I only care about you.

Sara: Did I mention I love you? I'll have to kiss you when you least expect it.

Malorie: I love you, too.

Sara: I just realized something. I miss you when you are away. I wish we had some classes together. We never get to hang out. You look cute when you're mad. Did you know that?

5/9/02

You won't believe what happened yesterday. Sara came over, and we walked down to the tennis courts. We were sitting on a bench talking, and, as I was in the middle of a sentence, Sara kissed me. It wasn't very long, but it lasted maybe 3 seconds. I was taken off guard, but I enjoyed it. The whole time we were walking around, we started planning our futures together. We talked about going to the same college, and she said that we were lucky to find each other so young. She told me that one day it would be possible for us to get married. She told me it would be hard to find a pastor who would marry two girls, but we would absolutely try a Christian wedding. She told me she would wear a tux and that Rachelle would be her best man. I was so happy she'd let me be the bride with Marisa as my maid of honor. She told me that we should have the ceremony in her back-yard and adopt children. (Sara lives in a beautiful manor house in the middle of nowhere with acres of land. She even has her own bush maze/labyrinth in her yard.) I can't believe how happy I am. I never knew I could be this happy, and she tells me she feels the same.

5/11/02

Today was my cousin Kelly's wedding. I was a junior bridesmaid, but I could barely focus on the ceremony. I kept imagining Sara and myself getting married. I could see us up there saying, "I do."

God is with you all the time and should always be in your life no matter what- even if you are gay. He will still love you. I've decided that. Despite what many I know think, I believe fully that this is true.

Also, Sara just called me. Her parents overheard her saying that she loved me. They had a big discussion with her about why she shouldn't be a lesbian, and she just agreed with them. She thinks she convinced them that they misunderstood her and that we aren't together at all. I'm not sure if they believe her or not.

5/17/02

Sara and I kissed three times today. We went to the bathroom at lunch, and no one was in there, so we kissed.

5/19/02

I am so happy. I am in love. I have true love. It isn't a crush like before, it's real love, and if this isn't love, then I will never know what love is. I feel great. We French kissed, and it felt great. And I wasn't nervous. No nerves. No fear anymore.

5/24/02

I'm spending time with my family in Georgia for my cousin's graduation. There's a lesbian couple that is friends with my uncle, and I think it's great that he's both religious and accepting of that. I wish my parents would be the same way. They are not. My mom told me that they make her uncomfortable. She feels like they may be looking at her "that way." I asked her if she thinks all her friend's husbands are looking at her "that way." It didn't go over well.

5/29/02

Sara and I spent the day hanging out at her house, in her pool, and around the grounds of her house. Gosh, I love her so much.

6/08/02

This is going to be long and hard to write. It's my 14th birthday. Sara has been 14 for 6 months; I finally joined the club. It is my birthday and, not to mention, the worst day of my life. It all started yesterday at the 8th grade assembly day. We had our assembly, and I got the "Charger Award" for being in the top 5% of my class of 2006. I got it for leadership, citizenship, and good grades. At the field day, we were all winning prizes, and I became a coat rack for everyone's stuff. They threw their jackets and prizes on me as they all scattered to play games. And I looked like an idiot being stuck with everyone's stuff. Then I told Sara that I felt stupid because she received so many awards, and she told me that I should feel stupid because she's "really smart." It hurt, but I ignored it.

Then, later that night (last night, rather) was the eighth-grade dance. Everything was fine until the last 20 minutes or so. Damian asked me out. Sara said, "You should go out with him. It's a good cover-up for us." I told her I could never do that to either of them. I love her, and I can't lie to the world or to him. I wouldn't put him through that, either. I care for him, and I had a crush on him before. I won't do that to him. Then everything was fine until our sleepover.

Sara, Rachelle, Lacie, Mary, and I had planned a sleepover at Sara's for after the dance. When we got back to her place, Sara and I went into Sara's room while everyone else crept into the pool. She cried to me, exclaiming that she was afraid she was going to lose me because Damian liked me, too, and I assured her that she was crazy. I asked her if she wanted to break up because of what she said about me dating Damian, and she replied back, "Of course not. I will always love you. I could never want to break up with you." I told her that I would never leave her, and she promised the same.

After we joined everyone in the pool, we watched "Moulin Rouge," and it showed me how much love could hurt. I guess it was foreshadowing. Her parents thought it would be fun to make us breakfast at 12am, and we all went to bed at 3am. That's when the first problem started. My nose was so clogged that I couldn't sleep, so I fell asleep at 3:30am.

Today ... today ... my birthday ... is the day I've felt the most pain in my life. I want to die. I feel like I will never be happy again. Mary woke us up at 7am, and we all decided to get up. Sara had disappeared. We couldn't find her. So, we went around the grounds of her home looking for her. The other three girls went outside to find her, and I stayed inside to check it out. Shortly after I began looking, she walked out of her parent's room, and I told her the scoop. We went outside to look for everyone else, and she told me that she told her parents everything about our relationship. She had to tell someone, and it felt good to get it out and let them know. As we stood on the front steps of her home, she broke my heart.

She said, "I can't do this anymore. I'm not ready for this. Can you imagine the hell we would live in if the word ever got out about us? People wouldn't understand. I just can't do it. I love you so much, but I can't put myself or you through this. But we'll always be best friends. I'm just not ready. Are you hurt?"

"Well, yeah."

We were still standing awkwardly on her front steps, and it was taking everything in me not to cry.

She continued, "I'm so sorry. I'm just confused and lost, and I can't deal with it right now. But I do love you more than anything in the world. It's okay if you hate me and ignore me for a while. I'll understand."

"Of course not, I know you will come back to me when you find yourself. And if you choose me, I'll be here." I'm not sure how sincere I sounded at this time.

"Yeah."

"*Do your parents hate me?*"

"*No! My mom even said that she kissed girls when she was our age and tried it out.*"

Honestly, I didn't feel anything. I was so hurt I could have died right there. We just weren't close for the rest of the day. I was disconnected from everything.

She added, "Oh yeah, I can't go to your house today like we planned."

We were both silent for a while. Deep inside, I knew she did love me like she said, but her parents were what did it. Just the night before, she was telling me that she would never break up with me and ten hours after, she was breaking up with me. She should be able to make her own decisions. They ruined our future. But, for now, I don't fear. I know that if she truly loves me, she will come back. Eventually. No matter what they say. Anyway, I'm in my dad's car right now at the party he's DJing. I was so excited to come here with Sara, but now I must be frightening him. I'm just lying in his car unable to move. I told him to let me be in here because I haven't slept.

The worse part, I was so shocked that I forgot it was my birthday. At 11am I remembered and exclaimed, "Oh, crap. It's my birthday." Sara looked at me with terror in her eyes and said, "Oh, God. I'm so sorry." I refuse to think of this anymore. It's in the past. We broke up.

6/15/02

She told me her parents said we could continue our relationship when she turns 15 if she makes that choice.

For now, they have sent her to therapy to "work out her feelings." I know what that means. I can only say I'm so glad they didn't talk to my parents about anything. My mother and stepfather would die.

We also must avoid each other for a while, as her parents don't want us to hang out or have sleepovers. This sucks. I'm thinking about how I'd have to tell my parents one day. I think my dad would be okay, but my mom would kick me out of the house for sure.

7/2/02

Okay, I've talked to Sara on the phone the last couple of days, and she is making me feel terrible. She's making fun of me, acting like she doesn't care at all anymore. She's acting like a different person. Did the therapist change her and make her suppress herself? Today, while we were talking on the phone, she kept calling me "fruitcake" and "candy girl." She was making me feel bad about myself for being gay.

Then I started talking to her online: Do you still like me? You haven't really been talking to me about anything.

Sara: I've been busy. I like guys.

Me: What do you mean?

Sara: Okay … I'm going, bye.

Me: Look, you've made it clear that you don't really like me anymore. Do you still want to go out when you turn 15? You keep changing your mind and sending me mixed signals. Do you still love me?

Sara: Mal, I told you. I am very confused right now. In fact, all I know for sure is that I'm staying away from both sexes. My mother was right. I haven't figured out my sexual preference yet, and I'm not going to blow it for either of us. I know I love you as a friend, but I don't know what love is. Be patient with me as I figure this out. Maybe it will be you. Maybe it won't. I have no idea.

Well, Sara is an insensitive person who changes her mind all the time. We went out, and she told me she loved me every day. She made the first move, always. I went at her speed with her making the first move, and sometimes it felt too fast for me. But I loved her and trusted her. Then her parents made us break up, and she told me (only a week ago mind you) that she still loved me and wanted to be with me as soon as she turned 15. Then she went to therapy and her whole mindset just changed? That's ridiculous. Since then, she keeps talking to me about guys and this guy and that hot guy. And then, "I love you so much like before." And then "I don't know how I feel." Confused? Yeah, I'll say. Obviously. But this game she is playing with me is killing me inside. I guess it's best to distance myself from her. We are going to different high schools. Perhaps it's for the best.

She's writing a fan fiction book. She made a fictional guy as the love interest for herself that she's obsessing over in the story. And she has made my character in the story weak, sniveling, and stupid in it. Why would she send this to me? I think it's clear that she doesn't like how I make her feel.

I wrote a bunch of responses, but I can't get myself to send them. I cannot wait for her and need to cut her out of my life, but this is going to be hard.

8/9/02

Sara came to my birthday party (which was held a few months late) and kept bossing me around, calling me her servant, and getting short with me whenever I did anything. She's bullying me; perhaps because of how I make her feel. Obviously, the therapist put her against her own feelings, and she's conditioned to hate me because she's suppressing her feelings. She'd keep sticking her tongue out when I'd look at her, but it seemed like she looked at me like she did when we were in love. Everyone said she was trying to be the center of attention, but I can't help being apprehensive and curious about what will happen when she turns 15 in a few months.

2/1/03

Sara's 15th birthday came. We went to laser tag ... and nothing happened. She ignored everything. I won't bring up anything again, so I think it will just be laid to rest. I'm okay with that, though.

2/19/03

I'm feeling an emotion that I haven't felt since Sara and I broke up ... happiness. Freedom. No more depression. I'm sorry that I haven't written in a while. I've been lifeless and upset. We've been in the middle of a snowstorm all week, and Sara came over today since we were out of school. At first, we stayed here and just talked about Buffy, and she gave me this pretty necklace as a late Christmas gift. Then we went to the park like we used to. (That's where we had our first kiss.) Sara and I talked about how great it was that we were exes and still friends after all that happened. That pried into the subject of crushes. I told her that I had a crush on this girl from Chesterfield last month, and she got jealous. That encouraged her to say, "You would never have feelings for me again after what I did, would you? I know I was terrible to you."

I paused … "Yes. I do. I'm sorry if that disturbs you, but I will always be honest about my feelings."

She used that to declare that she still had feelings for me, after all this time. She missed me the whole time but was afraid to tell me after the way she had been acting. All the pain I had suffered, she supposedly suffered just as bad. We were both relieved to find that we were still in love, but there was a problem. How would it work? I couldn't think she would hide it from her parents after what happened before, and they were still against it despite what they had said. And my parents would never understand. We decided we would work it out and try it, regardless. It was like Romeo and Juliet- two people together in a society that didn't want it. We walked back to my house holding hands, and we kissed. She told me she didn't deserve me after what she did, and I felt it had to be a dream. She told me that we should put a plan together to hide it better and figure out how we could see each other without people knowing.

She kissed me and then said, "We're screwed." What a weird thing to say. She still can't truly accept that this isn't a bad thing? Love is never a bad thing.

2/22/03

I have to say, I am the one needing to figure out my life now. Reflecting on the other day … all I've wanted for so long is to get back with Sara We got back together, and I thought it was all I wanted more than anything in the world, but I can't feel anything. I was on a high the other day, finally having gotten what I wanted for so long. But then she said that we were "screwed." What a funny word to refer to love. She kissed me, and it's like the spark is gone. I don't feel anything anymore. It feels wrong when being with her felt so very right last year. Can it be that after all she dragged me through the last 8 months or so made me fall out of love with her? I didn't think it was possible. I spent 8 months longing to be with her only to for it to feel wrong when we kiss now? This is what I wanted. But why doesn't it feel right now? And she keeps saying that we need to take is slow and that she's scared. Can I be with someone who is afraid to be themselves? Will she keep dragging me through the mud with her? I have a lot to think about.

2/23/03

I feel like I'm dying inside. Like I've betrayed my dad. He's never done anything bad to me. I'm one of the joys in his life, and I feel like he doesn't look at me the same- like he's disappointed. He tried to hide it, but I can tell. I told him about Sara: our past and that we still like each other, since we may get back together. I really love my dad, and I trust him to keep my secret and love me no matter what. He told me that no matter how I turn out he will always love me. That I didn't do anything wrong (though now's the only time I feel bad about it because he knows). He told me he thought I would end up with a guy, but he would respect my choices still if I didn't. I'm glad I told him, but I'm afraid he's disappointed in me. My dad's the only one who can understand me. I'm afraid of my mom and stepdad and could never tell them.

3/1/03

My dad has been incredibly supportive, and he really cares. I love him very much. Unfortunately, I was lying to myself saying how happy I was that Sara and I were back together. I just can't feel for her anymore. After everything she put me through, the spark isn't there. And I wanted it to be. But I can't feel anything anymore. So, it's over. For good. She's too insecure about who she really is, anyway.

So now I move forward with the support of my father. I'm glad I could be honest about myself with him, and he is supportive. And, as far as Sara, at least I know that she gave me the confidence to be myself. She gave me the strength to find out that I can be confidently gay and not be afraid that God won't accept me. I am me. And I am happy with myself. I hope she learns to be happy with herself. Love isn't a bad thing. It's a good thing. You just have to find the right person.

***

Fifteen years later, I am married to a man. I found that I love regardless of gender, and that is a wonderful thing.

Looking back on Sara, fifteen years after everything happened, I see that it was definitely not a fling or a phase. I had discovered a part of myself that was there and will always be there. I discovered that I am capable of love without gender, racial, or any other bias to anything other than who a person truly is in their heart. I think that's beautiful.

I hope that young people can learn from my story and see that love is never bad. It's a beautiful thing, though sometimes it might not seem that way. Everything happens for a reason, and finding the person you will spend the rest of your life with is a gift. The journey you go through to get there, and the loves you experience on the way, are all blessings that teach you who you really are and who you will grow up to be.

Embrace that, and enjoy it.

Since I Fell for You

Flo Golod

We were neighbors.

My roommate Paula and I moved into the shabby upstairs duplex during the winter of 1973. As March melted the snow and eliminated the need for obscuring hoods, we got a good look at the downstairs couple as they walked their shaggy white dog.

Harry, the dark-eyed husband, left early every weekday with coffee and a belt of tools.

Green-eyed Lena, a vision in long waves of red hair, rented the garage behind our duplex where she made huge *objects d'art*, constructions of metal and wood combined with painted canvas that reminded me of war zones, or aggressive sexual encounters. She banged around in there all morning after Harry left with his tools.

Industrious Paula, a graduate student engaged in the study of the rise of the nation-state in Europe, was impressed with the discipline of their lives. She arose every morning at six, made coffee, read the paper, ran for forty-five minutes, showered, ate, studied and left at twelve-thirty in the afternoon to labor as a teaching assistant until five in the evening.

As the mornings grew warmer, Paula told me that she and Harry bonded over coffee and the paper on the front porch. A shade-tree mechanic, she was interested in how things fit together. Harry was a recovering graduate student. He'd abandoned a Ph.D. about a Chinese dynasty for the certainties of physical labor, and the autonomy of self-employment. They shared a fascination with the imposition of order.

I was the odd duck in the order department. I was more or less engaged with a study of women in utopian communities. Also, more or less engaged in an affair with my advisor, a philandering socialist whose main virtue, from my point of view, was that he didn't care whether or not I ever finished my research on women in utopian communities.

That summer, I wasn't doing anything about women in utopian communities. My advisor was on a sabbatical in Bologna, probably seducing the women he interviewed regarding their collective buying clubs. I was proof-reading for a living, working at home, and only when I felt like it. I had plenty of time to observe the habits of Harry and Lena.

One warm April day, I came home with a manuscript to read and food to cook. As I edged through the screen door onto the porch, Tai greeted me with enthusiastic jumps, tripping me, so the groceries and unbound manuscript scattered all over the porch. Harry yelled at him and helped me gather the escaped tomatoes, eggplant, and plums.

While we were crawling around the porch, Harry scanned the words on the far-flung pages enough to determine that I was reading a manuscript on 17th Century China by a prominent professor.

"Are you a China scholar?"

"No, I'm not an anything scholar, at least not right now. I'm a proof-reader. These are publishing proofs."

"He's publishing this? I don't believe it?"

"Well, he's the head of the History Department. The university is publishing it."

"Unbelievable. Un-fucking-believable."

I must have looked taken aback because Harry stopped his excavation under the couch, where the bibliography had landed and sat up on his haunches. He gave me a huge smile and said, "I'm Harry, your neighbor, and I used to be a graduate student in 17th Century China. I hate this guy's work. I won't bore you with the details. I'm sorry about Tai."

Harry was, and probably still is, unbelievably handsome. Dark hair, dark eyes, and a nice big Italian nose that made him practically exotic in the mid-west.

"I'm Lindy and don't feel bad. The professor is a dickhead, and I'll just charge him for an extra hour of proof-reading."

"Want a beer?"

"Sure. Let me put the groceries away, so they don't torture the dog, and then I'll join you."

"I'll re-collate the pages and try to ignore Chairman Dickhead's prose. Don't be long or I may kill again."

I did hurry back, and the beer turned into two, and Harry told me about his unhappy graduate school life and the frustrations that led him to ditch his doctorate. He talked about how much he loved building things, and how he was learning to do cabinetry from an old Finn who sang workers' songs, and how his parents were having more trouble accepting his trade that they were accepting his gay brother. Then he told me about Lena and her sculpture, and their mutual commitment to autonomy, and how important it was that he not interfere with her self-renewal time—one to five every afternoon after she came out of the garage—even though he always felt like talking when he came home at three, and it was hard to leave her alone, so she often went other places so they wouldn't be tempted to get it on or go to the movies.

I was entranced with the details of their arrangement, and with Harry who had the knack of flirting and being serious at the same time.

"So, tell me what you do when you're not proof-reading for Professor Prick?" grinned Harry.

I was telling Harry about utopias and women in them, and he was thrilling me with tales of anarchist grandparents who had sent his parents to the Stelton Modern School in New Jersey when Lena appeared on the porch.

She wasn't tall, but she carried herself with grace and authority. Usually, beautiful women intimidate me, but Lena was also a clown and another friendly flirt.

"Oh, Harry, you have a new friend. Good."

Lena straddled Harry on the couch, covering him with a waterfall of red hair and a long kiss. Tai joined the love fest, inserting himself between the red hair and Harry's outstretched arm that held a beer can, tipped and dribbling. I felt like jumping into the fray myself, especially when Lena turned and smiled, "I'm Lena, the one who makes the racket in the garage. Do you feel like you moved into a construction zone?"

"No, we used to live in an apartment building with neighbors named Zoner and Boneman, Hell's Angels. You're not even in the same league. Besides, you make noise in the morning, in the service of art, right? I'm used to noise at night, in the service of party-on and drug dealing."

"I should deal drugs out of the garage. Then we could go to China."

Deftly sliding himself out from under Lena, Harry rolled his eyes. "Lena wants to engage with the Great Wall, and then come back here and sculpt something that will run twenty-five miles along the Mississippi River and prevent religious war from breaking out between Minneapolis and St. Paul. While also promoting racial harmony and an end to the oppression of women."

"Irish Catholics vs. Swedish Lutherans vs. Everyone Else. Harry still hasn't embraced my vision."

"I don't want to go to China. I practically had a psychotic break when I saw the manuscript Lindy is proofing."

I explained about my manuscript and quickly dissociated myself from all matters of Chinese scholarship.

"Well, what do you study? You look like you study something?"

"Why? Because I'm pale and myopic?'

"No, you look, well …" Lena scrutinized me with her inviting green eyes, "You look intense and bohemian … and pale."

"I'm intensely not studying anything right now. I look bohemian because I'm poor, and pale because I read manuscripts at home when I should be riding my bike or improving myself outside."

"Well, you're a pale beauty. I'll ride bikes with you sometime during my self-renewal hours, and then we can both be freckled beauties."

I was flattered. My hair, also red, springs out in childish ringlets. My eyes are blue but obscured by thick lenses set in wire-rim glasses.

"Watch out that Lena doesn't force you off the road. Whenever the scenery overwhelms her, she forgets to steer. She ran me into a gully in Ireland last summer."

"You guys have parents in the airlines?" I asked.

"I get little art commissions, and then Harry goes and finds somebody who needs something built and we manage to make our way."

"I'm jealous. Proof-reading and utopias are no way to see the world."

"You're starting a utopian community?" asked Lena with matter-of-fact interest, as though I said I was starting a dry-cleaning franchise.

"No, I study utopias, not start them."

"She's doing women in utopian communities. I was telling her about Stelton," said Harry, getting up. "Anyone want beer?"

"I want wine," said Lena and glanced an invitation at me.

I shook for no, not sure if my light head was beer-related or the result of all the friendly sexy energy on the porch.

"Harry and I both have utopians in our family trees. My aunt lived in an intentional community in New York. She had stories to tell. Very complicated stories."

"I'd love to hear them. "

"Well, she's dead, so, I'll be your medium." Lena threw back her head and lowered her lids, 'Ze vision … ze vision … ze vision. Ze struggle is to keep ze vision in mine head when ze reality is no utopia."

Harry reappeared bearing a tray with two glasses of white wine, another beer and an inviting arrangement of cheese, crackers, and grapes.

"Oh good, a party." Lena picked her wine glass up by the long stem and handed me the one I thought I turned down.

Harry placed the tray on a pile of books, out of Tai's reach, passed around the treats, and landed back on the couch, throwing one leg over Lena's lap.

"She's doing Aunt Riva before the wine? Usually, it's Aunt Riva after one glass, and then Uncle Boris after two."

"Uncle Boris was a gangster and a pederast," volunteered Lena cheerfully. "The other side of the family."

We talked and drank until after dark when Paula came trudging up the steps, home late after a seminar. Harry invited her in to join us, and they commiserated about the details of furnace installment in the coop then under construction down the street. Lena and I talked about our families, and I told her about my affair with Morris, the socialist.

"There's something irresistible about socialists. All that righteous indignation must fuel the libido. I've been in love with three socialists, one Communist, though he was a bore except in bed, and a Trotskyite. "

"All before Harry?"

"No, the Communist and two of the socialists were before Harry. But the other socialist, Maureen, and Tim the Trot were during Harry."

As I carefully considered this information, Harry and Paula were agreeing that collective decision-making did not lend itself well to the installation of heating systems.

"So you and Harry have an arrangement. You see other people?"

"Yes, we see other people and, in my case, some of the people are women. Are you shocked?"

I was a little but wouldn't admit it. "No, it's just a lot to take in at once. I just met you."

"I felt close to you as soon as I saw you talking with Harry. He's rarely that animated with new people. You inspire trust."

"Well, that's nice to hear. Usually, I think of myself as inspiring jealous dependence or lust followed closely by indifference. Trust is a big improvement."

Lena smiled softly at me. "Self-deprecation and irony. A smart woman's defense of her broken heart."

"Well, cracked a bit but not broken."

"Am I prying?"

"I just told you my dark secret. Of course, you're not prying. But my love life, of late, is not that dramatic."

In the light of her thoughtful gaze, I felt shallow and exposed.

"You look sad."

"I've had a lot of wine and beer. I better go before I get maudlin."

I pulled myself out of the old wicker rocker, wobbling a bit as I placed the empty wine glass carefully on the tray, noting the hand-painted fulsome cupids engaged in something complexly erotic but hard to make out in the dim porch light.

"Good night Lena, Harry. Thanks for drinks and treats and talk."

Lena rose up in one effortless swoop—had she been drinking with me for the last two hours?—and wound her arms around me, burying her face in my shoulder and surrounding me with that wonderful hair. I felt her full breasts and strong arms and smelled lilac.

Harry got up and put his arms around both of us and kissed me, pretty definitely, on the mouth.

I might have swooned, fallen lightly back on the wicker rocker, were it not for the cradle of strong arms holding me up. Harry and Lena untangled themselves and leaned on each other, regarding me in a curious benign way, I smiled, first at Harry, then at Lena, then at Tai and then at Paula, who frowned over her beer.

Slowly I made my way up the dark stairs, leaning heavily on the rail. Once home, I pulled my clothes off and fell into bed, knowing I'd be up in the middle of the night to pee and brush my teeth. I was fading as Paula came in, turned on the living room light and then clomped into the kitchen to make herself a salad, her ritual delayed—but not destroyed—by the generous attention of our neighbors.

That night I dreamt that I slept on a huge bed in a vaulted loft in the mountains. I lay with my arms around Tai, blanketed in waves of vast surreptitious pleasure.

Through the cool spring mornings, I committed myself to order. I got up at six-thirty and drank coffee on the porch with the paper, Harry and Paula who was surprised by my sudden return to order. Harry and I exchanged *bon mots* about the morning news as he left to hammer and saw. Paula then ran and returned to ponder nation states. Lena decamped to the garage. I claimed the porch for my morning study and proofed the treatise on 17th Century China, then another on the chemical basis of schizophrenia, and moved into a study of urban architecture and the reclamation of female space by June, as the mornings grew warmer.

I can only proof-read for an hour or so at a time. While the others pursued their callings, I found my way back to utopias and started reading and scribbling again. Some days I could feel the ardent pulse of the communes beating with the conflict and steely determination of the effort to live intentionally.

Then, after a time with my utopians, I'd return to other people's academic obsessions and proof on till lunchtime. Lena and I established a routine. I'd get lunch together. She'd emerge dazed from self-absorbed creation, dusty and ravenous. After a quick shower, she'd fall on the sandwiches. Somedays, I'd put her off with an appetizer, and we'd bike to the river and eat our picnic close enough to hear the splash of Minnehaha Falls, the squeals of small children and their mothers' warning calls, but far enough to have a few willow trees to ourselves and the illusion of privacy.

On the porch or at the falls, we'd talk and talk, an endless inquiry into our own natures and speculative analysis of everyone else. Lena scrutinized Harry's character endlessly, blaming his torture over his failed studies and limited capacity for friendship on his striving mother, or his cold father.

And Lena's paramours, the socialists, the artists, the actors, how she found them, how they worked things out in bed, whose bed, who else they loved, who got hurt and why, and Harry's watchful vigil until the fling ended. Lena's affairs were conducted mostly between one and five in the afternoon. If she weren't having an affair, she'd go to a yoga class or have tea with one of the ex-lovers or a lover of an ex-lover, and they'd talk about art and politics and sex.

Lena pried me open that summer. I told her about my affairs and the boy I'd loved in high school who drowned in Lake Superior before we got up the nerve to sleep together. Lena believed this was a formative event and accounted for my unconscious decision to abort all romances by picking men who would die, metaphorically, before I could love them. We'd lounge on the couch, and I'd rub her feet, sore from the hours on the garage floor. Or I'd put my head on her lap under the shade of the willow tree, and she'd braid my hair and laugh because she said I looked like Raggedy Ann, only more intellectual.

One day she was fiddling with my hair, and I was describing the confusing years before my mother was finally committed. Lena was softly rubbing my forehead when a sudden eruption of shouts followed by a spray of sticks, leaves, and pebbles came hurtling at us.

"Filthy dykes," bellowed a hoarse adolescent voice and we saw three boys racing through the trees. One, a little guy with blond hair that stuck up in a cowlick, stopped and gave us the finger, then raced through the trees after his friends.

Lena laughed and started picking the wet leaves and sticks off her shirt and my hair. I was red-faced, scared and humiliated.

"Why are you laughing? That was hideous."

"Sexual repression in America. They're just babies."

"But they're practicing hostile male violence. In a few more years they'll be beating up gays in parks."

I was shaking, and my voice was shrill. Lena removed a wet leaf thoughtfully from her blouse and put her other hand on my face, pulling my gaze firmly toward her.

"Are you upset because they called us lesbians?

"No, I mean yes. They called us dykes. It's not me personally, or not us, I mean. It's just the idea of that much hate, that much ..."

Before I could expand, Lena pulled me over and kissed me on the mouth. I stiffened for a second, then put my hands on her rib cage and returned the kiss. More kisses on the mouth, then on my face and her neck. Kisses on shoulders, my hands found her breasts, her hands found my thigh. We necked for a long time until childrens' voices reminded me we were still outside.

I pulled away. "Those boys might come back. Let's get out of here."

Lena smiled indulgently and casually circled my left nipple, still hard under the light cotton blouse. I felt an absolutely sickening thrill of wetness and helpless love from the spot on my breast, down through my intestines, drenching the inside of my panties and weakening my knees.

"Let's go, Lindy lesbo before you melt."

"You're a laugh riot."

I gathered our stuff together and shoved it into my backpack, avoiding Lena's eyes. We walked back to our bikes and started home. The late afternoon traffic kept us both alert and, for once, Lena didn't try to bike next to me and talk. Harry was right, she often forgot to steer, and she'd forced me off the road more than once when pointing out a natural wonder or holding forth about important matters.

I was glad to have an excuse to not talk and just concentrate on surviving rush hour. When we pulled up to our duplex, Harry was just leaving to walk Tai.

"Where you been ladies? It's after five."

"We were accosted by dreadful boys in the grip of homosexual panic and Lindy had a nervous episode. I had to comfort her."

I couldn't think of anything to say, and I think I looked guilty. Lena looked victorious. Harry looked dubious.

"Want to walk with me?" The invitation was extended towards us both, but I knew it was meant for Lena. This was their usual time.

"Not me, thanks. Lena, I'll put your bike back. Go walk with your guys." *Pretty damned suave,* I thought.

Lena handed me her bike. I was holding mine by the bars and hers by the seat, about to push them to the garage when she stepped between, trapping me.

"Don't let those mean boys get you down. We're too advanced for sticks and stones." She cupped my face in her hands and gave me another long kiss.

I stiffened but this time didn't melt. Harry, after all, was standing there watching.

Lena let go of me and patted both my cheeks, then backed up and went over to Harry, tickling his cheek and scratching Tai with the other hand. Harry's hands were clenched, but as Lena returned, he unlocked himself and winked at me.

"Don't let Lena over-power you. Save yourself."

"What should she save herself for?" demanded Lena.

"For me," he grinned and kissed Lena. Then he grabbed her hand and steered her off towards the park. Tai ran around them in circles as they moved away from me.

Dizzy, slightly nauseated, I wobbled the bikes back to the shed, locked it and dragged myself up the back stairs, beautiful new wood planks that Harry built for our landlord. I ran a tub full of water, hot enough to turn me pink. I found a bottle of brandy under the sink and poured a shot into a snifter.

Edging slowly into the tub until my body could take the heat, I slid down to my neck and started inhaling brandy fumes, then taking generous sips. The brandy was gone before the water cooled. I heaved myself out of the tub, paddled water tracks and drips all the way back to the kitchen, grabbed the brandy bottle, and dripped back to the tub. I was pouring myself a second snifter when I heard the screen door slam and Paula's voice.

"Hello."

"Hello, I'm in the tub."

"Can I pee?

"Sure, come in."

Paula came in and landed on the toilet behind me. I didn't turn to look but just waved a hand in greeting.

The brandy bottle was on the floor, the almost empty snifter on the edge of the tub. I felt an aura of disapproval fill the bathroom.

"We're decadent tonight."

"Yes, we're decadent tonight. Don't ask."

Paula flushed, left and I could hear her banging around in the kitchen.

I shut my eyes and thought about the insides of my mouth, my breasts, my neck and my thighs. All the places Lena had been. Then I thought about the places Lena hadn't been yet, and my insides got hotter than the tub water. I had no words, no analyzing thoughts. Only drifting, stupefying desire.

In July, Lena went out east to visit her family. Harry had a big contract remodeling a kitchen and couldn't leave. He worked long hours and usually didn't come back to our duplex until early evening.

He'd smoke dope and read, sometimes we'd hang out, and he'd fold early.

"I'm a dull boy," announced Harry, "Let's have a date on Saturday night. We'll go see Last Tango in Paris."

I'd been avoiding the movie. I'd heard about the butter scene and was feeling squeamish.

"Oh, come on," teased Harry, "You can cover your eyes, and I'll tell you what happens."

My objections were ritual anyhow. I was dying to go out with the handsome Harry.

Saturday night was hot, windless, almost airless. I found a dress that weighed nothing and swirled in soft cotton drapes that left most of my body free of cloth. Harry wore one of those Indian cotton shirts and a pair of clean jeans. Tanned and alert from a day of no work and no dope, he looked fabulous.

We walked to the theater. Harry draped his arm over my shoulder and held forth about the depredations of Nixon. People eyed us as they passed; we looked good and sounded smart.

The movie had a strange effect on me. I felt depressed and vaguely ashamed. I turned my head into Harry's shoulder during the butter scene while he made a big point of giving me a blow by blow account, loudly enough to annoy the reverent cineastes in the audience. The tango, at first, faked me out. It seemed to signal a better time, softening him, defining her. But when the very young Schneider shot Brando, I felt sick.

I grumbled my objections to Harry on the way home. He took my hand and listened patiently.

"Lindy, it's a stupid, pretentious European flick. Sound and butter, signifying nothing."

I thought it signified plenty and none of it encouraging, but I wanted consolation and let it go. We held hands and didn't talk for a while.

When we got home, Harry announced his intention to nurse me back to good cheer. He put a record on, Gato Barbieri, the Brazilian saxophonist who'd provided the soundtrack for the movie.

"The only redeeming feature, for my money," said Harry. He knew about jazz, something I had only lately discovered, still getting over rock and roll.

Barbieri's sexy sax melted away the bad vibes from the movie. Harry lit candles, turned off lights, found some stuffed grape leaves, cold white wine for me and dope for himself. I drank my wine. Harry smoked his joint.

"Now, for the healing powers of Harry's hands," he announced, and gently pushed me back on the mattress covered with an Indian throw that functioned as their couch. Harry began to expertly massage my feet.

Although my feet didn't hurt, the massage, the wine, the candles and the saxophone made me relaxed and expectant. Harry rubbed my feet for so long that his hands took on a character of their own and I stopped thinking about Harry the person, the handsome man, the husband of Lena and gave my feet over to bliss.

"You're not going to sleep on me, are you?" Harry had let go of my feet, moved to my side, taking one limp hand and placing his other on my shoulder.

"No, not sleeping, just melting. Thanks, Harry."

"The third rule of seduction is not to put her to sleep."

"What are the first two rules?"

"Place her in jeopardy and then save her."

"You saved me from Last Tango. Of course, you insisted we go."

"Exactly. Peril. Rescue."

"Rule Number Two?"

"Minister to her every need, create trust and dependency."

"Wine, candles, food and foot rubbing. Very nice, Harry. Truly suave."

Harry grinned his wonderful grin. I found my strength and reached my arms up and around his neck. He dove into my neck, nuzzling my shoulder, my ear, my hair. Nuzzling led to kissing, and I rolled off the mattress and onto Harry.

I had on only the cotton dress and underpants. Harry's hands were all over me, expertly and easily but I couldn't get at much of him. The shirt had to go over his head, the jeans had five snaps.

"You're too easy, and I'm too hard," observed Harry.

"Is that a metaphor?"

"No, literal truth. You're wearing one piece of diaphanous gauze and underpants that I could slip off with one finger. My clothes require concentration and dexterity to remove."

I lifted myself off Harry and back on the couch bed. Harry applied his skills to removing his clothes. I was so interested in the confident, tuned-up male body emerging that I just sat and watched.

"Do I have to do everything?" asked Harry, reaching down from his naked height to the hem of my dress."

"Yes, you do. I'm so impressed with the performance that I'm gosh darned near helpless."

Harry laughed and pulled my dress over my head. He tossed it down, and as promised, got my underpants off without any apparent effort.

Harry was skillful and careful. I was so relaxed that none of the usual anxieties of sex with a new somebody interfered and I felt like the best dancer on the floor.

Sex with Harry was affectionate and absorbing. But afterward, he jumped up abruptly, murmuring, "Be right back."

I heard him pad into the kitchen and open the fridge. He came back with the wine.

"Back in another minute." He headed into the bathroom, and I heard him peeing. When he emerged, he announced, "I'm going to let Tai out and roll another joint."

"Why don't you paint the ceiling while you're at it?"

Harry smiled absently, ignoring my sarcasm.

When he finished his errands and returned, he sat at the edge of the bed, rolling himself another joint.

"Everything simpatico?" he inquired.

"I'm fine. Are you always this busy post-coitally?"

Harry's hands stopped, and he looked over at me.

"I'm sorry, Lindy. First night jitters." He smiled reassuringly.

I didn't believe him. Three-rule seducers don't have jitters, especially afterward.

"I'm not sentimental, but you know, it's nice to lie around for a bit and chat."

Harry's brow furrowed, and I could see him taking my point. He put the joint on a dish, moved the wine and lay down beside me, wrapping his arms around me in a big, apologetic hug. We kissed and one thing led to another and pretty soon Harry was on top of me and inside of me. My well-rubbed feet curled tightly, and we were rocking away. Afterward, Harry sighed and moved off me slowly, carefully arranging himself next to me, gently tugging his free hand through my impossible hair.

"*Tres Bien*," he said.

Harry has nice manners and winning ways, but I felt like I'd just been congratulated after a tennis match. I rubbed the hair on his chest and lifted myself up off the wet spot and out of the circle of sex energy.

"I'm going upstairs, Harry. It was a lovely date. Seduce me again, sometime."

Harry grinned, widely and fully, obviously relieved to be off the hook for conversation.

"Night, darlin'. Should I see you to your door?"

I laughed, "No, I think I can find my way."

I found my dress, forgetting my panties, and made my way through the familiar kitchen out the back door, up the stairs, and into our kitchen. Paula too was out of town, so I had our place to myself, a blessing since I wanted no attention in my muzzy state.

I heard a thin version of Last Tango, without the sax. Harry was out on the porch, whistling to himself and probably finishing the interrupted joint, petting Tai.

Fifteen feet above him, I slipped off to sleep in my own bed.

Lena came back in a bad mood, uncharacteristically one she didn't want to talk about, saying only that it was vaguely Oedipal. She congratulated me on my tryst with Harry,

"Harry needs friends. He talks to you more than anyone but me. Maybe you'll prime the pump, and he'll branch out more."

I wondered if this meant that Harry would sleep around more in search of friendship and how, exactly, this would all work out. I also felt vaguely condescended to, but I couldn't formulate a protest. I wondered if any part of Lena was jealous.

After a few weeks, Lena's mood lightened and our afternoon ritual resumed. She had a new commission and was busily engaged in making something large and incomprehensible in the garage. She said she didn't want to talk about it, but unlike the Oedipal problem, this mystery made her happy.

We went swimming in the hot August afternoons. If it was too hot, we went to the movies or a cool bar. And talked and talked.

One night I had an actual date. I'd been proofreading a manuscript about bugs and the environment in Baja California. The fellow who wrote it, an entomologist, was nice-looking, straightforward and seemed uncomplicated. We were going out to dinner, and I wasn't even nervous because he was so nice and it was interesting to know someone who thought about bugs all the time.

Lena helped me get dressed and sent us off with a maternal smile. It was a perfectly satisfactory date with no pressure for sex. I was coming up the walk feeling just fine until I heard the shouting. I froze at the front door, hearing Lena screaming, "You have to act like you care, Harry. I don't know if you care unless you tell me, show me. I can't relate to an abstraction."

"Lena, I tell you I love you every day, twice a day. We fuck all the time. I take you places, buy you things, promote your art. What do you want?" Harry sounded aggrieved, desperate.

"I want more, more, more. I'm not ashamed of wanting more. I want a passionate engagement. I want you to be there for me."

"Lena, talk about abstractions. Be there. I'm here. What the hell else do you want?"

Lena burst into tears, and I could hear her sobbing. Harry made mollifying noises. I backed away from the front porch and crept around the side of the house and up the back stairs. I felt extraneous, unwittingly intrusive. I heard noises that indicated the fight was being made up in bed. All the good feelings from my old-fashioned date had drained away and been replaced by an incomprehensible stew of anger and jealousy.

I couldn't sleep that night. It was hot and still, and I felt suffocated, stuck in my bed, stuck in my life.

I was so lost in my own confusion that I didn't register the little scrabbling noises at first. Slowly, the scratching sounds filtered through the internal roar of my crisis. Someone was throwing pebbles and sticks at my window screen. I got up and moved behind the curtains, trying to see out without being seen. I wasn't scared, just puzzled.

A stage whisper hissed through the dark, "Lindy, it's me, Lena. Open your window."

I opened the screen and learned over, laughing, "Lena, what are you doing in the tree?"

"Shh. I want to talk to you. Harry's sleeping. Come out. Please."

"Just come up."

"No. I don't want to come up. You come out here, we'll go in the garage."

It seemed like a grand idea. My bad mood evaporated, I put sandals on and crept quietly down the stairs, across the yard to the garage.

Lena was standing in the door, looking wild-eyed. She folded both her hands over my arm, "Oh, I need to talk with you. I thought you'd never wake up."

"I wasn't sleeping. I just thought the noise was the wind. But then I remembered there's no wind. What's wrong, Lena. You look whacked out."

Lena was pushing me gently toward the back of the garage, steering me around the big thing which looked like a dinosaur in the dark.

"I need to talk to you. Harry doesn't understand. He tries but he just can't. Or won't. I can't tell if he's being a lout or just a dunderhead."

I thought that was kind of hard on old Harry, but I didn't really want to talk about him anyhow, so I left his reputation to fend for itself.

"Look, I made us a nest."

Lena had a tiny little desk in the back of the garage. A lampshade, one of those red fringed numbers, made everything look lurid. Next to the desk, she'd wound an assortment of Indian spreads, old afghans, a couple yards of velvet, and a black silk sheet around a beanbag chair.

"There's wine too. I took it from the house." Lena was pouring the half-empty bottle of red wine into two old chipped coffee cups.

"Join me, please."

I lowered myself into the tangle of cloth and Lena folded herself next to me. She put her arms around me and lay her head on my chest. I took a gulp of wine, then abandoned the cup to the floor. I put my arms around Lena, and she started talking. She talked about her father, about Harry, about some guy she'd been stuck on when she first met Harry. She talked about how much she liked men, how much she hated them. She loved Harry, but she hated his passivity. She loved her father, but he always stayed just out of reach.

After a long time of this, I asked, honestly curious, "What is it you want from them, Lena?"

"I want more. I don't want to have to say it, define it, I just want it. I know you understand because you have it."

Lena pushed my hair back and pulled my face toward her. I didn't know what it was, any more than Harry did, but I felt I had it all and more, an abundance of feeling, love, and passion, enough to make Lena satisfied and happy.

Kissing Lena and exploring her breasts, I felt willful and greedy, as full of unguarded desire as I ever had in my life. I swirled my hands around and around her breasts, fingers tickling the nipples.

Lena pulled my t-shirt off, so I was naked except for the sandals. She had a pair of Harry's boxers on, but the shirt was long gone. My thin tight body felt ripe, covered in a soft wet sweat. Hers felt hot and firm. I wanted to run my hands over her for the rest of my life.

New to women, I got sort of stuck on Lena's breasts. After a while, she held my hands still and said, "There's more you know."

I knew it, but I wasn't sure what I knew so I didn't say anything. Lena looked down at my crotch, half hidden in the folds of the nest. Her hand gently pushed my legs apart. She smiled at me and slid her hand down between my legs, her fingers gently circling tender spots. I melted, literally, wet from waist to knee and dripped excitement all over the nest and Lena's hand. I was so overwhelmed by my own pleasure, I forgot about Lena's body for a minute and let my hands rest limply on our legs.

"You too, Lindy. Put your hand in me, too."

We got the boxers off, and I plunged a hand down between Lena's strong legs and inside her soft places. I know knew how explorers feel. The terrain has never been walked on before, but it's been anticipated for so long that the place seems both familiar and wildly new.

My hand explored for a while, and then I found the places that moved her, followed her sighs, her pushes, her groans, and did what seemed to make her happy.

An exchange of hands between legs, up and down hips, over stomachs, back to breasts, then down into pubic hair and sliding fingers gently in and out, then tongues, first hers, braver and more knowing, later mine, tasting carefully, tentatively.

Later on, after she climaxed, I came, then we both came again. We lay there tangled in wet sheets and legs and arms, and it occurred to me that the rest of the world still existed, that there was a context for this nest and that it would soon demand something of us.

Lena was humming and telling me how soft and sweet I was and how happy she was and was I happy and how did I feel. I felt glorious, ecstatic, filled with wonder and awe. I was also terrified, sure that we were about to be exposed, chased from the nest and banished to our respective rooms. Instead, I said, "I'm groovy."

"You're groovy? That's all you can say?"

"I could go on and on, Lena. Please don't make me express myself. I'm overwhelmed."

Lena relaxed, looking pleased. Clearly, overwhelmed was a satisfying response.

"The first time can be so intense, yes, really overwhelming."

"Do you mean the first time with anyone, or the first time with a woman?"

"Oh, I mean the first time, just the pure intensity of that first time. When it's with a woman, then it's just more intense, more of a first, first time."

I had no idea what Lena was talking about, but I didn't want to get accused of not being there, so I just looked at her while she expounded.

"You know, you're drawn to someone's surface persona, then you seek their sexual self, their secret ways … and then the whole thing becomes more than the sum of its parts, and you're just really with someone ... into them, and you're no longer separate, but together you're something more than yourselves. Then when the sex is over, and you're back to your surfaces, you know what's throbbing just below that surface. That's when intimacy starts."

I wasn't sure if Lena was talking about us, or orating about sexual matters generally. I felt like a bit player in her erotic narrative. I loved Lena, surface, and insides, and didn't really understand the diagram of intimacy she was drawing. I wondered if I was short of the scale, insufficient. I felt a little chill and pulled a throw over my shoulders.

Lena sensed my confusion and wrapped her arms around me, tightening the throw around my throat.

"I go on and on sometimes. I know what I mean, but I can't always make it accessible to anyone else. That's why I do this." She pointed up at the metal dinosaur looming over our little nest.

I'd forgotten about the thing which now looked frightening. I wondered what it thought of us.

"Lena, it looks menacing."

"It does, doesn't it. I didn't realize I was working towards menace. I felt like a warrior fighting the metal for meaning. But now I think as I fill it out, it'll be less harsh, you'll start to feel the longing, the anguish."

"I just hope it doesn't eat me and then feel anguished."

"It's not rapacious. I won't let it consume you. Then there'd have to be remorse, and I don't want remorse. It's not part of my emotional vocabulary."

"Never?"

"No, never. People hurt each other, and they have to heal each other. Remorse is for drunks and wife-beaters. It's not part of a natural, healthy human exchange."

I seriously doubted this, having felt remorseful about weekly and feeling a little remorseful now, on Harry's behalf. I wondered why Lena opposed it so. Before I could think the better of it, I asked, "Lena, what's going to happen now?"

"Now, you mean right this minute or what's going to happen to us now that we've made love in the nest?"

"The nest is what I mean. What about Harry? What happens next?"

"I'll tell Harry. He'll be a little tight at first, but then he'll understand."

"What will he understand?"

"That this friendship is so intense it had to be consummated."

I wondered if, now that we were consummated, would there be some kind of bedroom farce ahead with me creeping in and out of their bed and each of them finding their way to mine on alternate days of the week. Or if this was it, love was made, and now we went on as friends with the sex out of the way, the tension released.

I was afraid to press Lena further. I didn't want to be a pest, and I wasn't sure what I wanted, other than more Lena. I said, "We better go inside. It must be almost morning."

"It is morning. Look." A small skylight that Harry had installed in the garage roof framed a square of pale dawn. Lena turned the lamp off and the garage filled with that first thin natural light. The dinosaur looked less menacing, more hulking and pathetic. The nest was a mess, and Lena looked pale and tired in the morning light.

She picked my t-shirt up and pulled it over my head. I held my hands up and let myself be dressed, like a little kid. She found Harry's boxers and pulled them on. As the garage absorbed more of the light, I stared at her breasts, huge pale globes. I wanted to lift them up. Lena sensed my obstinate desire and brushed my arms with her hands.

"It's time to go to work Lindy. Lust will make you lazy. "

I thought it might make me insane.

I handed Lena a piece of velvet to wrap around her shoulders. Neither of us could remember what shirt she'd been wearing.

Lena led the way around the big thing and opened the garage door to sounds of birds and distant traffic. I followed her through the yard to her door. She opened it quietly, slid in, turned and waved through the screen, softly sliding away into the kitchen and toward a sleeping Harry. I trudged up the stairs, forgetting to be quiet, not really caring about discretion. I picked the paper up, opened the door and threw the day's bad news on the table. Exhausted, I knew I'd never sleep. I made coffee and moved around the kitchen with heavy, weighted feet.

I didn't care who slept or didn't sleep downstairs.

***

Fall brought everything to a melancholy impasse. Every couple of weeks, Harry presented himself for a night out, or in, with jolly talk and athletic love-making. After a few dates, the force of my indifference overcame the force of my passivity, and I started finding excuses. The first time I said I couldn't go out, meaning have sex, Harry looked a little taken aback but recovered with a quick grin and a wry remark about being, "Aced out by the bug man."

My feelings for the entomologist were indefinite and unexamined, but he was a simple solution to a complicated problem, so I encouraged more dates. After the first turn down, Harry asked only one more time and looked relieved when I said no again. We still joked and talked and got on as well or better than we ever had.

Lena and I didn't fare so well. The colder weather put a damper on the afternoon outings, and we didn't seem to connect so well in my apartment, knowing that an increasingly watchful and disapproving Paula would come home soon or that Harry was downstairs pretending to occupy himself.

Some days we'd still fall into long, intense conversation and find ourselves wrapped around each other. But whenever this happened, Lena diffused the glow with a joke or a maternal remark about my physical and spiritual well-being. She'd talked me into a yoga class and was taking a proprietary interest in my improved posture and heightened powers of concentration.

I longed to ask what was up, fantasized the brave question, the defining conversation, and the long sweet love-making. I dreamed of running away with Lena, but the fantasies stopped with a guilty snapshot of Harry's face or some unshaped dread, murkier and even more frightening.

On Halloween, Harry and I were carving a pumpkin at their kitchen table when Lena banged into the kitchen waving an envelope around and shouting, "Harry, Harry, I did it, I got it. We're going to Turkey!"

"Sweetheart, it's Halloween, not Thanksgiving. What's up?"

"Don't be a joker all your life. We're going to Turkey. Remember the fellowship I applied for? Way last winter. I got it. I'm an Ornstein Arts Fellow."

"Oh damn, I forgot all about that. Hoo haw. We're going to Turkey. What a gal. What a fellow!" Harry grabbed the pumpkin lid by the stem and cocked it at a jaunty angle near his head while he waltzed Lena around with his other arm, singing, "For she's a jolly good fellow, For she's a jolly arts fellow. She's an Ornstein Fellow. And Turkey here we come."

I'd never heard about the fellowship, I couldn't believe that Harry and Lena were exulting about up and leaving me.

"When does it start?" I asked, trying not to sound obviously plaintive.

"I don't know I didn't even think of that," said Lena.

"Give me the envelope, please." Harry grabbed the official-looking envelope and pulled out a sheaf of papers.

"Dear Ms. Green," he read, "Congratulations, you've been selected as one of ten Ornstein Fellows in the Arts for 1974. The Ornstein Foundation will provide you with a $10,000 stipend plus travel expenses and lodging for you and your spouse. Fellows must begin their fellowship-sponsored activities by January 10 of 1974."

My eyes strayed to the wall calendar, and I started computing the days while Harry and Lena resumed their jolly good fellowship waltz around the kitchen with Tai jumping up to join the dance party. With the holidays and travel time, I'd probably only have them around for another six or seven weeks.

Harry extended an arm for me to join the waltz, the invitation, offered with the usual Harry *bonhomie*, alerted Lena to my outsider status.

"Lindy, we'll miss you so much. I want to go to Turkey and make great shapes, and I want to stay here with you and talk and talk and talk." She wrapped her arms around me.

I wanted Lena to say she wanted to take me too. Harry moved his eyes from Lena's embrace of me and stared out the window, looking uncharacteristically solemn. I stood with arms at my sides, receiving but not returning Lena's consolation hug and I looked at Harry, aware that I had no idea of what he might be feeling about leaving home, leaving me, taking Lena away from me, ending the fluid us.

Lena's eyes, buried in my hair, looked somewhere else that, I sensed, rearranged me into the shapes she would make during the continuing project of creating herself. Harry was a given, a solid constant fact of her existence. I suddenly grasped that I was part of Lena's narrative now, but that I had no reciprocal capacity to sustain the story of us without the actual her.

November dragged along, bleak and dry.

"We need snow," shouted Lena towards the window. "We want a pillow; the earth needs a blanket." We all needed cushioning, from ourselves, from each other, from the jagged anxiety about what was next.

Lena was on the phone continuously, making arrangements, handling the red-tape of the fellowship. I was surprised by her sudden efficiency. Harry devoted himself to a last big job. Tired when he came home, he didn't stop for grass or conversation, but moved right into sorting and packing. Harry was cleaning up their present; Lena was charting their course for the next adventure.

I sloughed through the days and nights in a dull haze. I found some undemanding proofing to do, and the entomologist went off to Baja to scrutinize a beetle that lives only there. Paula was gone too, studying nation-states in Italy for the fall term. I had only myself to consider and too much time to contemplate my lonely irrelevance. A moon with so little tidal pull that the planet it orbits moves slowly but powerfully away to another part of the universe.

Harry and I got on well. Less jokey and charming, I found him more real. He looked sad sometimes. I was helping him sort out books and box them up. I got to keep everything he didn't want and sell it. Since I was proofing only enough to make ends meet, this was a deal.

"Go ahead sweetheart, take 'em all. Buy yourself something nice," Harry slurred his words in a mediocre Bogart imitation, using his marking pen as the cigarette. I made a face and Harry put down the marker and took my hands. "I'll miss you, Lindy. You're a friend, in a way my best friend. I know this has been confusing. Things get complicated. But I'm sorry to say good-bye."

I'd never heard Harry say this many personal sentences. I couldn't look at him. He was my pal, but I wanted him to simply not exist so that I could launch myself against Lena and declare my love, my need, make my own demand for clarity and promise. Still, I loved Harry and knew how difficult what he'd just said was, how painfully foreign such declarations were, knew I could help him out with a hug that would let him know I cared and that I wouldn't extract too much or make this too hard. But I couldn't help Harry or myself. Confusion made me cruel, and I couldn't preserve the part of us that was Harry and me. I couldn't look at him, or I'd cry, so I stared at the books and forced a joke.

"Aw shucks, Harry."

Harry looked hollow. He'd said something honest and sweet, without irony, and I'd abandoned him. My joke erased the risk and the truth of the moment, leaving only a deep desire for escape.

I kissed him on the cheek and escaped gracelessly from the basement. As I passed their kitchen on the way up the back stairs, Lena saw me and hailed me in. She was on the phone, shouting to someone in Turkey about the cost of a cottage.

"Yes, we want a comfortable cottage, too. But we are on a budget. Please find one that costs less." Lena rolled her eyes and made the greedy sign, rubbing her thumb and fingers together in the air. I wanted to leave, knowing I couldn't pretend attention to anything except my own misery, so I kept my hand on the door handle, signaling intent to leave. Lena turned the finger routine into a full arm invitation, waving me in dramatically, like a circus barker, pointing at a bottle of red wine on the table, miming a toast with deep quaffs, and all the while, repeating her budgetary concerns to someone on the other side of the globe.

My resolve melted and I was in the door, wiping out wine glasses, pouring wine, handing Lena a glass while she finished.

"Oh, very good. That sounds excellent. Yes, send me the rental contract. At the American address. No here, not the Foundation office. They give me the money, and I'll send your money as soon as I read the contract. Yes, right away. Thank you. Goodbye."

"Good golly, Miss Lindy. That man was impossible. He wanted to lease us a ten-room 'cottage' that would have cost most of my fellowship. He thinks we won't be safe in only three rooms."

"Did you get what you wanted?"

"Yes, I'm very good in these situations. Harry and my father are always surprised, but I can handle bureaucrats and greedy hustlers. I know what I want, and I don't waste time on people who get in my way. I'm polite, but I persist and push through obstacles."

I felt oddly aligned with the distant agent. Except that my greed was muted, suppressed by fear of rejection. *If I wanted money, would it be easier to ask?*

"Lindy, we haven't talked. I've been so busy, but I think about you all the time. We have to talk."

"What do you want to talk about?" I could barely get the words out.

"Us. You and me. Our time together. And now, our time apart."

I clutched my wine glass and stared into the redness, hoping to find the right words, just by looking. I started crying, making no sound.

"Oh, Lindy. I'm so sorry. Come here."

I didn't move, so Lena came to me, pried the wine glass out of my hand and wrapped her arms around me. I cried into her hair, trying to hold back the sobs.

"It's all right Lindy, you need to cry."

I knew I needed to cry, but I didn't like Lena prescribing for me. I wanted her to cry too, both of us washed in grief, desperately clinging to each other, refusing to be parted. Inconsolably glued to each other. Who would try to separate women in such a state?

I pulled myself away from Lena and grabbed the wine glass, downing the red liquor that coated my aching tongue and throat.

"Why do just I need to cry? You don't need to cry? Don't people cry for orphans? Why don't we put my picture in a magazine? 'Only a dollar a month will find this woman a home. You can help.'"

I'd found my voice angry and spiteful. I was shouting and crying, hoarse but clear. Lena pulled herself away and regarded me with appraising eyes.

"Lindy, we're your friends, and we're moving. People move, move on. It's part of life."

"Oh, give me a break Lena. Friends. Gosh, let's keep in touch."

"Well, friends and lovers, too. Of course, it's painful. People always fight when they're getting ready to say good-bye. If you're mad at someone, you don't have to face how much you're afraid of losing them."

"Oh, Lena, please don't be so wise. Just say good-bye and go."

I turned and left, drained but relieved. I went upstairs, made tea and found a jigsaw puzzle that Paula had left. A thousand pieces of the Coliseum. Suddenly, I felt like accomplishing something. I put records in a stack on the stereo, everything—Janis Joplin wailing her losses, Graham Parsons reminding me unnecessarily that love hurts, Joni Mitchell being smart, and the soundtrack from West Side Story. I sat at the table, drinking tea and patiently putting the ruin together. Letting the records drop, one by one.

Finally, it snowed.

The city muffled under that first clean blanket. We made up. Lena apologized for being absent and for anything that might have sounded condescending. I apologized for being touchy. We all three got dressed up and went out to dinner. Back in their kitchen, we hugged in comradely fashion and agreed that I wouldn't come down in the morning when they left.

Lena cried, and Harry smiled fondly at me, placing a consoling arm around Lena. I gave them both quick kisses on cheeks and took myself up the stairs.

The moonlight bounced off the new snow on the garage roof and filled the dark kitchen window with soft, diffusing light. A few pieces were missing, so I couldn't finish the Coliseum. Incomplete, the ruin glowed through the cracks in the puzzle.

Mind-blowing

Pam Flores-Lowry

Ally had failed an exam for the first time. She was frustrated, furious with herself and mostly sad. She tried to use her walk to the bus stop as a sort of meditating moment. *Things happen for a reason. I can do this. I'll do better on the makeup exam. Positive mind, positive body. Damn, I hate being alone. I can't do well alone. I need a signal. Something to move on and forget about him …*

The minute she said the word 'signal' was the moment it started raining. *Awesome, worst signal ever.* Then, something else happened. A motorbike stopped by her side; its rider a bald guy with blue eyes. *The signal.*

"Hey, can I drive you anywhere? I'm Josh," he said.

"Oh, um, hi. I'm just going to the bus stop."

"Come on, I can take you there. I can't promise you won't get soaked with rain, but you'll get there faster."

"No, thank you. I'll walk," Ally told Josh.

"Well, I can't say I didn't try. Let me tell you something, you're absolutely beautiful."

"Thanks," Ally said, blushing a little bit. *Maybe it is the signal. What if this was the beginning of a whole new exciting adventure?*

"Can I least get your phone number?" Josh asked.

"Mm, okay," Ally yielded.

"And a name?"

"Oh, sorry. My name's Ally. Nice to meet you," she answered. She bowed, she didn't know where that came from, but Josh seemed to like it because he laughed.

"Nice to meet you, too, Lady Ally," he said and then held her hand, kissing it.

Josh saved Ally's number and rode away slowly. Ally was puzzled. There were no more thoughts about the exam, no more fears about failing. All she could think of was Josh and his crystalline blue eyes. She kept walking to the bus stop while texting her friends. "I just met the most handsome bald guy in the city!"

"Bald? Ugh," Laura promptly judged.

Ally was used to her negativity, so she didn't pay much attention to her answer.

Soon there was another beep, it was Karen. "OMG. Where? Send the address, I'm in need of one bald hot guy myself."

Ally read her friends' texts and laughed. They made the perfect group; each with her own dreams, strengths, and flaws. She loved them, trusted them. They were gold.

When Ally got home, she kissed her parents. She was in her third year of college and still visited them often because they lived near her dorm. She was thankful that her mom didn't ask about Luke. Luke and Ally had been together for two years, and they were on a break. Sometimes Ally's mom could get a little bit too intrusive, but not that afternoon. Plus, there was Josh to think about …

Just by a stroke of magic, her phone beeped, a message from Josh. "Did you get home safe? Josh."

"Yes, thanks, what about you?"

"Just started my shift."

"Oh, sorry about that. Do you usually work late?"

"Yep, I'm a bartender. You should come and check out the bar sometime."

"Sure, which one is it?"

"The Brewing Bar, the one on Main street."

"That sounds great. I might see you over the weekend, then."

"What about tomorrow?"

"I have classes the whole day tomorrow, unless you bartend from 2 to 3, my lunch break.

"I don't work that early, but we can have lunch near your campus."

"It's a plan, then."

Ally promised to text the address of a café the following day. She talked a little bit with her parents, joined them for dinner and left their house in the evening. As soon as she got to her dorm, she ran into Karen. She filled her in with the news. Karen started jumping in the air and suggested a code for the next day, in case Ally didn't like Josh.

"I can text you saying I have an urgent problem. Then, you get back with me," Karen plotted.

"Okay, and I'll try to text fast, if I ask you to call me, be ready to do it."

The following day was a Thursday. Ally got up worried, desperately looking for the right outfit to meet Josh. She decided to go for jeans and a white tee. After all, she just wanted to be comfortable by showing her true self; no need for make-up or high heels.

Her first classes were boring as hell. She tried hard to focus, but her mind was wandering around Josh. She kept looking at the time on her phone. When it was one in the afternoon, she realized that she never texted the address to Josh. *Oh my god, maybe he'll get here anyway, I mean, he does ride a bike.* Ally attempted to hide the phone so that the teacher didn't notice her texting.

Josh answered quickly with a brief 'ok.'

That was a little bit cold. Ally didn't know what to do with that 'ok.' *Is he mad at me? Did he forget about our date? Is he in bed with another woman?* Eventually, it was time to meet him, that is if he was actually there at Pebbles Café.

She knew she looked fine, maybe even hot. Ally crossed the street and saw him sitting outside in the shade. He waved. They shared a pizza, drank sodas, talked almost endlessly. She didn't know how or why, but it was so easy to talk to him. She didn't find herself without words, as it often happened to her. There were no awkward silences. Josh was fun and a good listener. In a nutshell, she shared information about her fears, dreams, studies, likes, dislikes.

He, on the other hand, talked mainly about his trips abroad or his job.

"Would you like to own a bar at some point?" Ally asked him.

"I'm not sure, I guess I'd need to finish my degree in economics first," he confessed.

"Oh, wow. We've been sitting here for, I don't know, forty minutes and you haven't mentioned you study economics. Which school do you go to?"

"I dropped out two years ago. I decided to travel, you know, I was 'in search of adventures.' Plus—" Josh was interrupted by a loud ring. It was Karen.

Ally had never answered her friend's text, so she called her. Karen was relieved to know that everything was okay.

After that, Josh quickly changed the subject. He wanted to know if he could see her again on Friday. He had to work, but maybe she could at least stop by the bar. She agreed without even blinking.

On Friday, as promised, Ally went to The Brewing Bar with Karen. She didn't have good memories of that place. A couple of years ago, she ran into who she thought was the love of her teenage life. She looked at the entrance, distracted by the music coming from the speakers, thinking about that guy, how we sometimes connect places with people. Ally's eyes went over the Irish decorations on the wall, and then, she saw Josh. She had to make her decision fast. Was she going to sit at a table or at the bar? Karen said that she didn't mind sitting at the bar, but she might look a little bit desperate if they sat there.

"Table for two," Karen said with an air of belonging to this place, even though she had never been there before. The hostess led them to a table near the patio. Ally tried hard not to look at the bar, she succeeded. After a few minutes, a server came to their table with the menu. They both ordered imperial stout beers. 'Imperial' sounded like their kind of beer, plus stouts were always a good choice. Little did Ally know about the real alcohol content in imperial stouts, because after drinking one single pint she walked straight to the bar.

"Hi Josh!" she said trying to refrain herself from kissing him.

"I thought it was you who entered a while ago! Hey, how are you?"

"Great, I just had the best pint ever. I didn´t even know I liked imperial stouts," Ally shouted.

"Cool, yeah they are really good. Did you come with your friends?"

"Yeah, I'm with Karen. I told you about her yesterday, I think, um, when she called me. She´s over there. I can't believe we´ve never been here before. I love the place," Ally said emphasizing the 'v' in 'love,' drawing attention to her lips, almost biting them.

"I know, it´s great. Hey, they have an opening right now, someone's about to leave, and we could use some help on the weekends. It can get really busy," Josh explained.

"Oh my, that sounds perfect, I'm actually looking for a part-time job right now," she said, not even knowing where her words came from. The truth was she didn't have time for a job, she had to study! In fact, any free time she had was probably better used for studying, damn, that feeling of failure still lingered on her.

"Awesome, I'll talk to my manager. He'll give you his card. We may even be coworkers soon," he joked.

"Sounds great. I'll come back to the bar before I leave then," Ally promised. She returned to her table with mixed feelings. Karen wasn't sure what to read on Ally's face, it was a mixture of success and defeat.

"What's going on? I thought you went to the restroom and then I saw you going straight to the bar instead. Any news about Josh? If he asked you to stay after his shift ended, sorry but I want to go home by eleven. Stop smiling, what's wrong with you?" Karen inquired.

"I think I just applied for a job here," Ally confessed.

"Oh my God! Does that mean I get to drink for free? Maybe just a few pints?" Karen laughed.

"Haha, really funny. I don't think I even have time to do that," Ally admitted.

"I'm sure you'll manage. I mean, I'm sure the money is okay, and what's more, you'll get to spend some time with Josh, make sure he's not a weirdo. No offense, but you did meet him on the street. He's cute and all, but you don't really know him. Although it seems like a lot of work to just get to know a guy. Maybe the lady is in love!!!" Karen kept joking.

"What if I'm in love? He's so cute! The fact that he rides that motorbike doesn't hurt either."

"Oh, my friend always focuses on a good soul, not a material girl at all," Karen said.

"I mean, you saw him, you can look at him right now. He seems like a good guy, exciting, full of adventures—" Ally kept going.

"Adventures you can start on his motorbike!"

"So funny," Ally told Karen while drinking a new pint.

"Well, he does look cute, and you need to forget about Luke," Karen reminded her friend.

Damn, Ally actually forgot about Luke until Karen mentioned it. *What if he found out about this new possible relationship? Did Luke ever go to The Brewing Bar? Did Luke's friend frequent the place?* She couldn't risk being seen flirting with Josh, but why was that? Did she still have feelings for Luke?

Luke was almost the perfect guy. He was thoughtful, kind, respectful … but sometimes that wasn't enough for Ally. She wanted risk, uncertainty, adventure. Luke was never capable of offering that, but there was one thing he could offer, safety. Ally always felt so safe when she was with him. She shocked herself when she gathered enough strength to ask for a break. Would that break lead to a break-up? And here she was now, free after all, able to date whoever she wanted. What was she going to do with her new freedom? Why did she still feel guilty when someone mentioned Luke?

Karen and Ally ordered a third round of beers. By the time it was eleven, they had already left The Brewing Bar. Karen walked with a buzz; Ally with a card in her hands.

"Should I email the manager?" she asked Karen.

"Sure, you get to hang out with Josh and get paid! It's perfect!" she explained to Ally.

"Well, the least I can do is send him my resume. Worst-case scenario, the manager may never call me, right?" Ally said.

Karen agreed with her. Sending a resume never hurt anyone. They took a cab to their dorm and went their separate ways.

The following morning, Ally woke up with a beep from her phone. It was Josh; he wanted to know if she had already contacted the manager. Ally was intrigued.

"Not yet, to be honest, I'm still in bed," she typed.

"In need of company?" Josh replied.

Ally felt embarrassed, then wrote, "just the good kind of company."

"Wait for tonight then."

"Fond of mystery?" she texted.

"Fond of you," he answered.

Ally kept the conversation going, and it gradually moved to more serious stuff. She promised him she'll send an e-mail to his manager soon. It seemed that the bar was in need of a new employee that same Saturday. It would be the perfect excuse to see Josh at night, by the end of their shift.

The day went by without any complications. She talked on the phone with Josh's manager, agreed to give it a try that night. Ally didn't have any experience bartending, but Josh's promise to guide her made her feel at ease. She wasn't so much worried about the job as she was about leaving the bar with him.

Around five that evening she headed to The Brewing Bar with a backpack. She was ready for an overnight at Josh's or wherever the wind blew, she thought. The job wasn't as easy as it looked. Too many beers on tap, too many people. Josh helped her in any possible way. She could feel the soft touch of Josh's hands on her waist whenever he moved to another side of the bar.

Many girls flirted with Josh, and this made Ally really jealous, but also confident at the same time because she knew she was the one leaving with him that night. There was something about Josh that attracted her, not only his body but his spirit. This whole idea of dropping out of college to follow your dreams, just travel around the world. She wished so desperately to do that. Then, her thoughts led her to her upcoming exams, so her mood changed.

When the shift was over, Ally got paid for the day; she was in a training period. She was ready to ride Josh's motorcycle, so she was surprised to find him walking towards a car. She didn't ask whose car it was, she just hoped Josh hadn't stolen it.

Once in the car, Josh started talking about his trips to Mexico and Hawaii. He talked about selling his shorts to buy pot from a local. Ally smiled, realizing how different Josh and she were. It pleased her. They started driving to his place.

Suddenly, he stopped the car in a badly-lit place. Ally stared at him, not sure what to do next. She had never done anything in a car, too aware of possible voyeurs. Josh grabbed her head and licked her lips with desire. Ally stopped thinking; her own body making all the decisions, getting ready for what was about to happen. She let herself go and enjoyed

Josh's kisses starting in her neck, gradually moving to her breasts.

The darkness helped her be present. She unbuttoned her shirt, removed her clothes, guided his hands around her body. Then, Ally made Josh unzip his jeans; she wetted her lips and got ready. Soon, Josh started sighing. She moved her mouth up and down with the help of her hand. Her tongue made circles around Josh. Ally had never felt so excited. Josh came in her mouth, making Ally feel ecstatic, powerful. Josh gave another sigh, looking at her like a man that had found a treasure.

"Mind-blowing," he said.

Ally smiled as if saying 'I know' with newly-found confidence.

"So, we, um, are heading to my apartment," Josh almost stuttered.

"Actually, I want to catch a movie tonight. Do you want to come with me?"

"I'd love to come and make you come," Josh said.

They went to the closest cinema. Ally was entertained by the movie while Josh kept looking at her every so often. Ally wasn't sure what to do after the film. She clearly liked Josh. She definitely enjoyed the adventure, the thrill of being in a public place. Luke would never do that. That's when it hit her. *Luke.* She might still have feelings for him. She needed to work on that.

By the end of the night, she called a cab to head home. Josh looked puzzled but didn't insist on her going to his apartment. He offered to give her a ride, but she declined.

"Sometimes I just like sitting on the back of a car and think about my day," she admitted.

"Okay, then, I'll see you at the bar," Josh said.

"I don't think I'll work tomorrow. I have a couple of exams next week," Ally explained.

"Oh, then I'll call you tomorrow."

Ally stood on her tip-toes and kissed Josh on the forehead to say goodbye when her cab arrived. She gave the driver her address and sat, contemplative, looking through the window. Outside, the night offered her new possibilities. Her mind wandered around college and Luke and Josh and the bar and the car. She had fun that night, but was that the kind of fun she wanted for the rest of her life? Did Josh and Ally have anything in common? Did they share any future dreams? Could they build a life together? Was it possible to have a better future with Luke? Did she need to focus on her studies more? Did she need someone reliable by her side? She decided to send two texts.

"I'd love to see you tomorrow," she wrote, and the other one read, "I'm thinking about you."

She sent the first text to Luke and the second one to Josh. Then, she typed again, "I can't get involved with you. You're fun, though. Have a nice life, Josh."

She pressed 'send' and paid the cab driver.

Here We Are

Ze Luiz

Oswaldo was staring intently at his muscular chest before draping his soccer jersey over it. He was analyzing a reddish-purple bruise that was developing above his right nipple. Ozzy, as most of his teammates referred to him, played fullback in the summer installment of the West Hollywood Varsity Gay League. Although it was sponsored by the Gay community, it was open to all. The league featured teams named after double entendres, such as Stranger Queens, Gayvengers, and Man Chest Hair United. Ozzy was part of the Messi Bottoms.

As a defensive player, Ozzy saw a large portion of the game's action and aggression, often coming home with bruised ribs or insteps. It was safe to say that he had bruised most surfaces of his body, and unlike his masculine mother, Maria Rosario, once told him not to worry, because gay men played like sissies, the gay men he played against were anything but.

"Osito," Mrs. Sampedro said, still calling her son Ozzy by his childhood nickname, meaning bear cub. "Those faggies you play with wouldn't be able to make a monkey come by spanking it."

"Ozzy, hurry the hell up, man," Nestor said. "Damn, kid. You take longer than a fucking chick to get ready." Nestor Bonavita was the team captain, twenty-two-years-old and acted as an older brother to Ozzy. "We're all waiting for you to start."

"Sorry, man," Ozzy replied. "I was just checking out this gnarly bruise I got in the last game."

Ozzy lifted his shirt to show Nestor the wound he was referring to. Nestor looked at it with squinted eyes, hummed a few times in various affirmative pitches, and began to poke the discoloration. At first with his index and middle fingers, then with all five of them, and finally rubbing it with the whole warmth of his hand. Nestor had big, strong yet gentle hands. The kind of strength that could make the bruise worse or better. Ozzy's flexed pectoral muscle fit perfectly under Nestor's healing hand.

"How does that feel, man?" Nestor asked as he rubbed his palm in a circular motion, at times, accidentally rubbing Ozzy's petrified nipple.

"Hmmm," Ozzy cleared his throat, not expecting to speak in the middle of this soothing process, having allowed himself to enjoy the therapeutic procedure his friend, brother and captain was using to make him feel better. "Sorry, I meant to say that it felt good. I mean, better." They locked eyes. "Yeah, it feels better." Nestor continued to rub deeply. Ozzy didn't want Nestor to think that the first sound that came out of him was a moan or that he was deriving the wrong kind of pleasure from it.

This whole experience reminded Ozzy of the time when he was six-years-old, playing at his dad's friend

Heriberto's swimming pool. Of how much joy he derived from the way Heriberto threw him up in the air and caught him in his big, burly hands, and how Ozzy himself would grab onto his hairy, corpulent shoulder, wet and slick from the chlorinated water. He felt a warmth, unlike the times his own dad played the same game with him a few moments later. There was something about Heriberto's eyes and smile that made Ozzy feel good, a goodness that he felt he couldn't share with anybody. A goodness that felt wrong to feel, but at the same time, felt so right.

A goodness Nestor's touch was pressuring his chest to feel.

"Man, your heart is pumping really fast," Nestor said, his eyes bulged in amazement. "You must be fucking pumped for the game." Ozzy smiled nervously. Nestor placed Ozzy's flaccid hand on his own chest. "Look." Nestor's heart was beating like raucous Brazilian drums amidst a capoeira bout.

Ozzy not only felt the pumping of blood in Nestor's warm chest, he felt just how firm and developed his pecs were. Ozzy had always admired them but had resigned himself to never be able to touch them. "I'm fucking psyched too, huh?" Ozzy swallowed saliva in order to buy himself time and not to moan again by accident.

"Yeah, you're really ready," Ozzy said, punctuating his fake statement with a false laugh to diffuse the awkwardness he had created in his own head.

"Alright, kid," Nestor said, tearing off his hand from Ozzy's chest and readjusting his crotch. "Let's go."

Nestor ran ahead of Ozzy who was lowering his jersey, continuing to rub his right pec, not out of hurt, but because it felt so good to retrace the rub work his friend had given him, running his hands through it as you would through wet sand.

On the field, Nestor wasn't only captain, he was the coach. He yelled throughout the game, alerting his teammates of incoming danger and possible goal scoring opportunities. Nestor breathed and lived soccer. Having been born to an Italian father and a Brazilian mother, Nestor's veins coursed with soccer. His cerulean irises would light up like two Olympic torches whenever an attacker approached him, placing his goalkeeper in scoring danger. Nestor was fearless. He was strong. He was a bully to the opponent. He was a fucking nightmare.

"Man up," Nestor yelled at his defensive line as three attackers approached his team's goal. Nestor's statement had a double meaning; it meant, mark your man as well as be as manly as you can be because shit's about to hit the fan if you didn't. Nestor hated getting scored on. He used to say that it felt like being bent over and taking it up the ass from a guy who didn't buy you dinner first. He would have a maniacal fit if Ozzy or one of the other defenders allowed or contributed to allowing a goal to go through.

Nestor led by example, taking balls to the face, stomach and to his own balls.

"I've got balls of fucking steel," Nestor would yell whenever the ball landed between his legs, doubling over most guys, but not Nestor. He was rock solid.

"Go, take it all the way," Nestor said as he recovered the ball and passed it to Ozzy, who was the fastest runner on the team. Ozzy was part of the track and field team during the school year, running mainly the 100 and 200 meters. His chest may have been lean, but from the waist down, Ozzy could have competed for Mr. Olympia. His quadriceps muscles were robust and well-defined, streaked with thick blue veins and shrink-wrapped with his tanned, deep brown skin. His calves were wide, like Hermes's wings, and allowed him to fly up and down the field, past defenders, with ease.

"Good run, kid," Nestor said. As the captain, it was Nestor's responsibility to also be the team's cheerleader and often displayed his affection toward his teammates by spanking their butts, picking them up as he hugged them—from the front and from behind—but Ozzy noticed that Nestor really liked the way he ran, in particular, and the musculature on his legs. "You've got an exceptional pair of legs, kid."

After most games, the guys would hit the community showers. Since they could only accommodate one team, the winners also won the right to post battle cleanliness. Ozzy never took advantage of this perk because he was only seventeen-years-old and the rest of the guys were at least five years older. He preferred to jog home and take a shower there.

"Hey man, don't be a pussy and take a damned shower with your boys," Nestor said after he saw Ozzy exiting the gym. He soon realized that Ozzy had never taken a shower with the team. "Come on man, even the gay dudes think you're fucking weird."

Nestor wrapped his muscular arm around Ozzy's neck, and that's all it took to convince him to stay. "Don't think of it as fourteen naked dudes taking a shower." Ozzy echoed Nestor's boisterous laugh. "Think of it as a legion of Roman soldiers washing off the mud and enemy blood after coming out of battle victorious." The thought brought a genuine smile to Ozzy's face.

"Okay, cool," Ozzy said.

As both boys walked into the showers, the other twelve immediately stopped their loud cacophonous conversations, cavernous laughter and distuned singing. It was as if an outsider had walked in, blinding them with the piercing, cold light of a camera, trying to document with an intent to display their privacy. Ozzy was stunned by the starkness in the room, having never seen that many men naked at once. The variety of body types, skin tones, sizes, and hairiness mixed together reminded him of abstract expressionism and the way their limbs interlaced as the men washed their soiled bodies, like cubism. Ozzy was taking it all in at once, not focusing on the two-bead flesh rosaries dangling freely between their legs.

"Hey fellas, stop staring and get back to washing your stinking asses already," Nestor yelled, half kidding, half commanding.

The group of men picked up their conversation as well as their soap right where they had left them before Ozzy's presence had disturbed their mirth and merriment.

"They're a bunch of fags, even the ones that aren't gay," Nestor joked. "Go on, take off your towel."

Even outside of the field, Ozzy heeded Nestor's instructions. Doing so made him feel pleasantly safe.

Ozzy hesitated for a moment, looking left, then right, the left again. He took a quick peek down at his towel, then at the men, then at his towel again. When he looked at the twelve again, he noticed a thirteenth body, Nestor's, had joined the Last Supper of asses and cocks.

"Come on, kid," Nestor yelled, gargling and huffing shower water cascading on his face. He waved Ozzy over to an empty shower next to his. "The water's real nice." Nestor's shivering smile was warm an inviting like that of his younger brother back when their mom used to bathe them together when they were three and four. It was also like that of Heriberto, the warm teddy-bear-man that made him feel so happy.

Ozzy undid the terrycloth knot that was keeping his towel up, one flap at a time. As the first flap moved away from his goose bump-covered torso, the gay constituency of the thirteen transfixed their fiery eyes on the denuding as if it were the unveiling of a new nightclub.

The second towel wing seemed to take a decade to flap itself to full-frontal freedom, but when it finally ended, Ozzy's penis placed another wave of muteness over Nestor's twelve Apostles.

"Damn, this dude is hung," a haggard voice with a forced effeminate twinge broke the silence of water dropping and draining. Everything in Ozzy's head was playing in slow motion. The 'u' in "hung" seemed to be ringing like a nail bouncing on the hard tile, whose rate of clinging accelerated faster and faster.

Ozzy's heartbeat mirrored this bouncing as twenty-four individual eyeballs analyzed and fantasized every inch of him.

"It looks like a fucking elephant trunk," a huskier, raspy voice yelled, starting a wave of laughter that drowned the whole room. Ozzy felt the tiled walls closing in on him, the steam boiling his blood, and the humidity sweating him into a piece of wrinkled jerky.

As he was about to bolt out of the room, he felt a strong grip take hold of his forearm. It was Nestor.

"Guys, just shut up, and let the kid take a damned shower," Nestor said. "God knows he's a damned good player, and the size of his dick shouldn't matter."

Nestor led Ozzy to the shower next to his, weaving and wading through a sea of nudity and whispered bickering, silent snickering and a little bit of dickering.

"Most of y'all look like you have clits between your legs, that sometimes I wonder," Nestor said as he and Ozzy arrived at the showers. "Don't listen to them. Fuck, I wish I had a dick as big as yours, kid. You're lucky. What are you packing down there? Eight? Nine inches?"

Ozzy's face flushed red, maybe due to the steam, but most likely to Nestor's compliment.

"I don't know," Ozzy replied in a small voice that didn't even sound like his own. "I've never measured it before." He lied. The truth was that he was too embarrassed to tell Nestor that his penis was, in fact, about ten inches long the last time he measured it, which was earlier that day.

Nestor's smiled at Ozzy's disingenuous ingenue. Ozzy giggled and smiled back.

"Besides, they're just teasing you," Nestor added. "Check this out. Hey everybody," Nestor grabbed his penis, hunched over, and began to scratch the top of his head with the other hand, the way a monkey would. The other guys broke out into a fit of laughter, holding their stomachs and pointing at Nestor's primate gestures, his gibbers and grunts, and the manner by which he was swinging and choke-holding his flaccid jungle vine of a penis.

"See? It doesn't matter," Nestor said laughing, slightly out of breath. "We're all just dudes."

Seeing Nestor's simian-samba sent an invisible jolt through Ozzy's body, especially when Nestor began gyrating his torso left and right, over and over, and the tip of his penis grazed Ozzy's upper thigh. In the midst of the hooting and hollering, he didn't think much of it, other than a mere accident. A happy accident, according to the smile plastered on his face.

After getting dressed in the same clothes he wore during the game, not having planned for this impromptu shower, Ozzy exited the gym and began to walk home. It was nearing ten-forty-five, and as he momentarily thought that it was perhaps a bad idea to walk home alone, Nestor steered his black Nissan Sentra by Ozzy, driving on the opposite side of the road.

"Hey," Nestor said, "Wanna ride?"

"Nah, I'm good," Ozzy said, immediately regretting having rejected his offer. "Thanks, though."

A car blared its deafening horn, flashing its lights at Nestor's illegally, idling car.

"You know that I don't like to take no for an answer," Nestor said, accompanied by The Beatles' "Come Together" playing in the background, smiling that charming smile of his. "Besides, I'm breaking the law for yo—"

Another car horn cut off the last part of Nestor's plea. Both boys closing their eyes during the duration of the painfully loud sound.

"So, what do you say?" Nestor asked.

"Sure," Ozzy gave in, annoyed by Nestor's unwavering cockiness, but pleased by his interest in him.

"So, where am I dropping you off?" Nestor asked as Ozzy closed the passenger side door. The smell in the car was a combination of wet Old Spice, pine car scent, and Nestor's chocolate protein shake breath. The delicate guitars of *Hotel California* by The Eagles began to play softly in the background.

"I guess on the corner of Fountain and Martel," Ozzy said, still unable to believe that Nestor was giving him a ride home. Nestor merged into the correct lane and sung out, "But you can never leave," right before the song went into the passionate guitar solo.

"You're Mexican, right?" Nestor asked. The question struck Ozzy as strange, but it also showed a level of interest.

"Yeah, my dad is Mexican, and my mom is Filipino," Ozzy replied.

"Cool, that's a nice mix." Ozzy could feel Nestor's fiery eyes looking him up and down. "As you already know, I'm half Italiano and half Brasileiro." The Italian and Portuguese accents used to pronounce the respective nationalities sent a warm shiver up and down Ozzy's back. It allowed him to relax into the back of his seat.

"So, do you speak Italian or Portuguese?"

"Nah. My dad bailed on my mom and me, and remarried another lady." Ozzy noticed that the joviality in Nestor's voice had vacated as soon as he began to speak about his dad. "My mom speaks very little Portuguese and she never really taught it to me." Ozzy kept looking over to Nestor's animated hand gestures, often lifting both hands off the steering wheel. It was a thrilling feeling, to see Nestor so excited and that at any second they could both swerve off into another car and die. "I did learn a few things from my grandparents back in Brazil, though. That's where I spent most of my summers growing up."

Nestor told Ozzy all about how these trips had awoken in him his deep love for soccer. A love that he pursued in high school and college. A love that came to a bone-crushing and heart-breaking end when he went for a soft tackle and the player he was running against went for a hard one. Nestor was carried off the field on a gurney, never to play again, professionally or at all.

"The doctors told me that I'd be lucky if I could walk again," Nestor said.

"Wait. How are you able to play now?" Ozzy asked, amazed at how good of a player Nestor was.

"It's all heart and soul, man. I refused to let that be my future. My reality."

Ozzy thought about his own disability, his inability to cope with the things that he often felt within his own body. To cope with his crippling shame.

"That's the only way to be truly happy, kid," Nestor said. "You just gotta grab life by the balls, and just take it and do what you want with it."

Nestor's words boggled around in Ozzy's head, and rang true in his heart, resonating deep in his soul. If there was anybody in the world that he could trust with his truth, it was Nestor. Ozzy closed his eyes. The car suddenly stopped. He took a deep breath. The Rolling Stones' *The Last Time*, stopped playing, allowing the silence of the streetlight lit night to fill the car.

When Ozzy opened his eyes, he turned his head to face Nestor, who was already looking at him with his azure eyes, as blue as Italy's national soccer team jersey. Ozzy saw Nestor's hand traverse the distant canyon between the driver and passenger seats, from Nestor's right thigh to Ozzy's left. Although his eyes told him that Nestor's hand was in the wrong, his innermost being told him it was right. It was the rightest thing he had felt. Ozzy began to feel lightheaded, the blood rushing to the lower half of his body. Nestor's hand gripped his thigh hard, borderlining an unbearable pain that soon morphed into an unbearable pleasure.

Nestor reached his left hand toward Ozzy's face, twisting his lean torso and leaning his face closer to Ozzy's. Nestor's touch filled Ozzy with a warmness he had never felt before. At first, Ozzy pulled back, inching away from Nestor's approaching pillowy lips. But Nestor's forceful hand pulled him back in for a warm, wet, hard kiss. There was a tenderness to Nestor's roughness. In the context of this intimate moment, his assertiveness made the moment unpredictable, as if anything could happen. As their lips met, Nestor let out a moan that Ozzy had associated with feral beasts. It was low and deep. This was Ozzy's first real kiss, having given up on the cause after a number of girls had rejected him throughout high school.

Ozzy opened his eyes to see what Nestor's busy hands were up to and noticed that the bulge in Nestor's tight shorts, the same one that he had seen bouncing up and down as Nestor hustled up and down the soccer pitch, was now bigger and sharper, concealing a third knee.

As the temperature rose in the car, Nestor's kissing became more animalistic, with the introduction of soft nibbling of the chin and neck, licking of lips and tongues, and hard biting of Ozzy's lower lip and shoulders. Ozzy wanted Nestor to consume every bit of him. Nestor's hand slid up Ozzy's muscled thigh, slowly, steadily.

"What are you doing?" Ozzy exclaimed, more out of reflex than concern.

"Shhh ... shut up," Nestor breathed warmly onto Ozzy's lips. "Let me take care of you, kid."

His words made Ozzy feel comfortable, safe. Nestor was, after all, looking after him, on and off the field. Before they had even locked lips, Ozzy was going to confide in him that he thought he may be gay. However, Nestor had read his mind, his body language. As their lips magnetized themselves together again, the ascent of Nestor's hand up his thigh resumed. It ate away at Ozzy's fear and inhibitions. Never in his short life had something felt so right.

When Nestor reached his ever-engorging penis, Ozzy's buttocks jumped off his seat for a moment, as nobody had ever touched it in such a firm yet delicate way. It reminded Ozzy of the time Nestor was rubbing his chest, of how he did so out of concern for his friend. He wanted to heal him. Now, Nestor wanted to heal a different organ, an organ that needed the most healing, one that needed more than healing, it needed deliverance.

Nestor began to stroke the shaft more lovingly than he himself had ever. When it came to masturbation, Ozzy would beat off to beat the clock. To beat his parents from finding out, he would do so without making a sound, or releasing a drop of semen, regardless of how hard he was. The pleasure he had derived from his deprived experiences had only been a fraction of what Nestor was making him feel now.

Ozzy felt conflicted, feeling good and bad, innocent to respond to the pleasures of his body and guilty to enjoy them all at once. Just as Ozzy began to get even harder, Nestor stopped. *Why did you stop?* Ozzy thought. Ozzy started to look outside making sure nobody he knew or didn't know was walking by the car. But they were alone. Nothing but blacked out apartment windows and the stars above. Before he knew it, Nestor began to pull Ozzy's shorts down, releasing faint notes of bittersweet sweat, the head of his penis getting partially stuck to the waistband.

"Damn, kid," Nestor said, "you are big." Nestor began to stroke up and down in a slow, rhythmic spiral. "I didn't realize you were uncut."

After Nestor licked his lips, he descended towards Ozzy's ticking time bomb erection and wrapped them snugly around it. The moist sensation of Nestor's mouth enveloping his virginal organ was foreign and intoxicating to Ozzy and flinched upon contact, like emerging into a warm pool of water, scalding at first but so comforting that even as the temperature falls, is so difficult to vacate.

"Relax, man," Nestor coached. "Just relax. I've got you."

Ozzy was afraid of what may happen if he did relax, if he truly allowed himself to feel good about what he had been taught to repress and feel bad about. Ashamed. The deeper Nestor plunged, the stiffer Ozzy's body became and harder Nestor stroked in order to make him release.

"Let go, motherfucker," Nestor yelled, as he did when he wanted Ozzy to run as fast as he could, down the field, leaving everything behind, including the belief that he couldn't defeat his opponent. "I know you're ready to come."

Ozzy let out an ear-piercing cry that made way for a warm wave of pleasure, consuming him from within, like the fires of hell his mother would surely say he would fry in for doing this with Nestor and feeling this way. Ozzy felt his heart pounding loud as audible clouds of steam were releasing from his and Nestor's mouths. The stiffness that had inhabited his body had left. All Ozzy could feel was a radiating heartbeat, pulsating from his legs to the crown of his head.

"That's it, man," Nestor said, "Give it to me. Just let it flow."

Ozzy felt his inhibitions flow violently through and out of him like rivers of living water, one spurt at a time. His closed eyes suddenly flipped open when he felt a hot moisture wrapping around his still erect penis. A feeling that he had experienced before when he almost drowned as a child. Ozzy looked down at his lap and saw the back of Nestor's light brown hair bobbing earnestly up and down, consuming his penis little by little, deeper and deeper like a river, a torrential Amazon that devours everything in its wake.

"I can't believe you're still hard, kid," Nestor exclaimed in laughing astonishment. "After I come, I'm done." Nestor kept jerking. "I need at least five minutes."

Ozzy was feeling good, happiness interlaced with guilt and a feeling of "what-will-they-think," looking out all of the car windows to see if anybody was out there. Anybody who could identify him. Out of nowhere, a heavenly blindness overtook his eyes, so unbearably pleasurable that all he could do was close his eyes and lean his head back onto the headrest. He felt the entirety of his penis inside of Nestor's Italo-Portuguese mouth, the tongue that had spoken a snippet of both languages so seductively was now doing to his penis what it had done to those words, twirling in circular motions around it, like pressing an orange onto a citrus juicer, wringing out the savory nectar.

He felt the exquisite pain of a second coming in the pit of his stomach and felt an undeniable need to release the contents of his body. To give up the ghost. As he did, he heard a choking, gurgling noise coming from Nestor and then a silent swallowing that Ozzy was only aware of because of the sensation on the tip of his penis.

As Nestor emerged from below, he began to inhale and exhale in the same way he did after having chased down ferociously after a fast attacker. 'It's the hard plays that make you better,' Nestor used to say. Ozzy felt he had just become a better person. A complete human being. Maybe not by having done something great for someone, but for the contrary. For allowing himself to be done something to and for having placed himself in this difficult situation with Nestor. A situation he had entombed, preventing it from happening or ever coming out in any way.

"Man, kid, you're fucking wide," Nestor said, choking and chuckling. "That was a huge load, by the way. Good job."

Ozzy looked down to Nestor, who was now resting his sweaty head on his chest. He pulled his chin up and kissed him long and tenderly. It was Ozzy's way of thanking him for helping him reach this new place in life, that of becoming a true man. He held his redeemer close and tight, enjoying him forever in that instant. Their interlaced bodies, Ozzy's dark skin wrapped around Nestor's light tone, were like swirls of milk and coffee dancing in an infinite spiral, slowly becoming one. Neither of them knew what would happen after that night. Things would go back to the normal that people used to hide a little bit of themselves. Sometimes a lot of themselves. Ozzy had dropped a load off his shoulders that night, but even in the midst of sexual and spiritual paradise, somewhere in his head was looming the load he would have to carry in the future. The battles he would have to fight against his loved ones and against ones who would never love him. People that would hate him for choosing to love another man.

At that moment, as Nestor's agitated breathing became gentler and gentler, he realized why this fearless leader and ravenous lover had never told him that he was indeed gay. All of that macho-ness that Nestor displayed was his defense mechanism against a queer world that wants all boys to be the same, to feel the same, and grow up to be manly men.

The sweat oozing from every one of their naked pores was tied to their secret, their shared truth, a truth that set them free. Ozzy and Nestor exuded confidence in the sexual act they had performed before no one, before the stars, before God Himself; not caring about sin, original or otherwise. Ozzy was reborn, resurrected, expelling guilt's poison, and the toxins that had welled up deep inside of him. Nestor helped him purify his soul.

But for that moment, Ozzy only wanted to focus on love. All of him was full of love. He simply wanted to love the man who had loved him. The one who had shown him how wonderful love could be.

Dirty Girl Diary: Misadventures of a Sexual Anarchist:

Nella The Chef

Valerie Taylor

"She went her unremembering way,
She went and left in me
The pang of all the partings gone,
And partings yet to be".
— Francis Thompson

This rarely happens anymore, but from time-to-time, I see someone that looks peripherally like her. When we initially broke up, I'd swear I'd see her walking down the street or rounding a corner. A familiar carriage or gate, possibly her profile or silhouette. It's a funny trick your emotions and memory can play on you—the slightest brush with a familiar characteristic and all of your past shared experiences come rushing back as if it were the present again. I'd fantasize that she was showing up to surprise me on a late flight from Florence or would call me to meet her at Blue Water Grill for oysters or even more far-fetched that she'd just show up at the door of my apartment one day. She swore oysters were an aphrodisiac—not that I needed any prompting—and were one of the most sensual and erotic things to share with a lover, and there were times when she'd actually cab it from JFK airport straight to the restaurant where I was to promptly meet her.

Our relationship began initially without much hubbub—a sum of the mundanities of everyday life incarnate. But I was wrong about the impact and influence this meeting and pairing would have on my life, like misjudging a wave while wave-surfing. Not thinking much of a wave, estimating that it won't end up turning out to be much, and then it ends up growing and increasing until it capsizes and takes you down into the undertow and sends you reeling and almost drowning. Like most things that end up changing the course of your life, it is barely even noticeable or remarkable at the time that it's transpiring.

Nella and I met while renting rooms in an Upper East Side brownstone. She was inordinately shy, demure and unassuming and I'm rather the opposite—my name is Francesca, but most people call me Fran, she used to call me the "obnoxious American" in an affectionately sardonic way.

My father was dying of cancer at the time, and I would stay up all hours of the night not unironically 'coping' by smoking out my window that faced a three-way brick wall. It essentially functioned as a chimney and an echo chamber rather than a window. I could hear the phone conversations of other tenants—couples fighting, laughing and fucking on the other floors of the building. What a view, and frankly that's how his impending death made me feel as well—boxed in with bricks coming closer like trick walls. I was slightly numb, and there was nowhere to go, like dying itself might possibly be. Incessantly and compulsively repeating game after game of old-school solitaire with actual cards on a physical, not a digital, desktop to deal with my simmering grief.

When my father was traveling for business as a CEO during my childhood, he would bring back different decks of airline logo packs of playing cards. An old-school giveaway for businessmen before airlines got so cheap when the bean counters realized they could save millions by giving five fewer peanuts per pack. Souvenirs from the road. Along with collectible iron-on stickers from every state he visited.

Later, when we would travel together to his real estate development in Mexico, Rancho Viejo or to other states to his historical restorations in the Midwest. We would pass the time together on the plane, side-by-side miniature back seat tables unfolded, him teaching me the "strategy" of solitaire. These childhood experiences on planes with him and spending long stints of time in non-American cultures may have instilled in me my love of travel and foreign lovers.

In retrospect, passing the time between my monthly visits to his deathbed in Michigan, playing this childhood standby of non-virtual solitaire, seems an apropos subconscious albeit slightly neurotic coping method.

Nella would come home at even odder hours than my 24-7 advertising studio hours. Leaving at ungodly early hours for prep work in the kitchen, at a time only farmers rose, while I was still up all night or returning back home from work in the wee hours of the morning when even the city that never sleeps was at least cat napping and eerily quiet except for the cycles of garbage trucks. That's the audible cue that you are up too late in NYC. So perchance, we got together based on my dying family member induced insomnia.

My room was situated at the front of the railroad apartment—it was a long hallway with alcoves for rooms. She always fussed with the lock for an inordinate amount of time, jingling and jangling her keys, in an obvious awkward struggle to open the door, no matter how many times she'd done it previously. This always disturbed me enough to awkwardly need to decide if I would rescue her from her sticky situation or not. Causing myself innumerable sticky situations in the future. She always rode a fine line between gangly, awkward misfit and sophisticated, highly educated world traveler—somehow being both opposite and distinct things at the same time—another manifestation of her bi-ness.

Gaining my attention with her antics and then gently knocking on my door and requesting me to rescue a maiden in distress, by bravely walking her to her bedroom at the back of the brownstone because she was afraid of the mice scurrying around due to a rodent infestation in this elegant place we called home. And this was typical NYC—overpaying for an outwardly highbrow address in a fire-trap multiple-code-violation interior. And that's even before factoring in the sexual harassment of the crotchety old Austrian landlord that shared our kitchen but with any luck, not our quarters.

He would shamelessly dotter back to our fridge in his underwear, down the apartment building open hallway, to store unidentifiable "body parts" as my other roommate Gretchen—the comedienne and temp secretary—called them. The fridge, a thinly veiled ruse to come to the apartment of four young women in different stages of undress. He'd given up on real relationships after unsuccessfully marrying and divorcing five times, almost the same exact story as my earlier 88-year-old neighbor in Florida, Bruce's doppelganger. He may have thought he was increasing his odds or betting on the desperate student paying off her rent with another form of payment. He usually chose isolated international students.

Gretchen and I were the American exception, which we made up for in good looks and potentially exploitable naiveté. He had countless reports filed against him, but somehow, he still let rooms for a living, a retired professor or academic, and sex offender.

All of us girls were so different from one another, but all, not coincidentally, good looking or for the plainer ones at least having nice figures. Rosa was from Peru—a tiny dark-complexioned woman with a straight and sharp bob, a peculiarly beautiful woman, unhappily overworked in insurance or a travel agency or some such droll business—a mini Cleopatra without the riches and prestige. She had the cheapest and most precarious hallway "room" with blankets and rugs over a clothesline demarcating her space. And this is the mildly and vaguely dehumanizing deprecation of cheap living in an inordinately expensive city. And she was a relatively educated professional.

Nella, the chef, hailed from Florence, Italy. Currently living in this rented room, our pretend "home," like a fellow transient, and like Rosa, our resident pseudo-Cleopatra, Nella clearly looked like misplaced royalty in the midst of this disrepair.

I later found out that she actually was royalty of sorts in her own right, by family renown, prestige, and money. She was here, on her own volition, earning her stripes on the battlefield of American French and Indian Fusion restaurants to return home to run the very masculine kitchens of one of the most generationally famous culinary families in Florence. She had to prove her stuff beyond her culinary pedigree. In the home—women can rule the kitchen because it doesn't pay, but as soon as it is lucrative, it's a man's world—exemplified by the Italian restaurant business. Her tentative lesbianism could have been a mild form of controlling the chaos of the gender paradigms of her culture or more likely a form of rebellion against them.

Partially she was in NYC as an excuse to be independent and shirk the robe of inheritance and to avoid, if only temporarily, the familial responsibilities she must at one point take on because of the tenets of her culture. Kind of like the Amish have their year of debauchery—I was her Rumspringa—and then she headed back to her community, perennially the properly reared, dutiful daughter. She was indeed raised well and wore her familial and social responsibilities on her shoulders like the Mandarina Duck backpack she never took off.

I always knew that the seeds of our eventual demise would grow in this soil, even when she vowed promises and plans to the contrary. Just like I knew, even as a little girl, that my father's advanced years when I was born, meant that he would never live long enough to see major milestones. Like his children get married, or graduate college or meet any of his grandchildren.

It was a knowing that would nag my conscience. I would swat away both these concurrent pangs of knowing like a horse swishes its tail at a pesky fly. I knew from the moment that we met, even though she didn't share this with me overtly, that she was stalling going back. Even when we moved in together, an outward beginning, I knew she was living on borrowed time. It was a desperate act of love and avoidance of forestalling the ending.

As long as she could stay, she did. We extended leases, I even bargained an illegal sublet down to buy her more time in the states by extending the money she'd been allotted. Yet, even though we came up with endless delays to circumvent her return back, the sand was running out of the hourglass. Her time here had run out, and history and politics hastened that end.

After being stuck in a basement kitchen working an early morning shift deboning fish or baking bread during the 9-11 terrorist attack and only having a Spanish radio station to listen to for information, she walked home from Chelsea to Washington Heights, over 160 blocks. Her father, who rarely visited this country, I think out of a distaste for it, borne out of a belief that anything that life offers is in Florence, so why bother leaving it? A belief that after you've visited there, you may come to agree with. He came over immediately and without delay brought her back home. 'Full stop'—one of her favorite phrases, which always reminded me of a telegram. That should have been the end of our love affair, full stop, an end to our tentative foray into playing lesbian house.

But the question of when to end a relationship is just like whether or not to start one. Sometimes, in retrospect, certain decisions weren't the wisest for either party, but I can't imagine doing anything differently if given the chance again.

Some endings are ill-timed—some are too early, and some too late—and some beginnings are ill-fated. Just like some affairs that never should have begun, like the pharmacist or the delivery man.

Sometimes I wish life was an app and had a do-over button like a board game and that you could play a "Do Not Pass Go" card. It's not so much a statement of regret *per se*—meaning I wish we hadn't continued on or I hadn't had certain relationships—but its an admission of wistful recollections that things could've gone differently if certain alternative choices had been made or levels of knowledge, insight or experience had been more equal.

Just like Shakespeare's free will within the bounds of fate. There is a point of no return when the choices get out of hand, and it culminates and accelerates to its ending. That moment similar to when you know a relationship is going to begin, just as when you know one is going to end.

But tsk-tsk, that would have been too easy, we decided to forge ahead based on our plans for the future. When I was done with school, I was going to move there and learn Italian, and we would have a kid together, me as the femme, the default carrier of this love child. It was a very ethereal, romantic and far-flung plan for our future. But we sincerely believed it, and even long-distance visit after visit to each other, I think we thought we were the exception to the rule that an ocean between us would never create actual distance between our hearts and bodies.

There is an inherent dopiness or egregious foolishness somewhere in the gestation of love. Part of all delusional enamoring with another is fool's gold. All that glitters is not gold. We think we are exempt when we love someone enough. But this is a false sense of security. The distance was increasingly romantic—yet inevitably toxic. For a very long time, she'd send me an envelope with a plane ticket in it. We'd travel back and forth at minimum four times a year plus vacations.

Nella had recently graduated from the French Culinary Institute and was exploring the different styles and approaches to back of the house dining. A self-appointed, but family approved, journeymanship of sorts, with their financial backing, to bring her findings back and apply her learning to her family business back home. Sometimes we would go together to get pastries at what she called "the porno bakery" because it was named Hot n' Crusty, she thought was raunchy. Her sensitivities and proclivities always embodied this paradox of nunnishness and finding the absurdity of the obscene in mundane things.

She was exceptionally sensually indulgent despite her reservedness—mainly this was expressed through food and erotic thoughts, but also in the bedroom. She said that my pussy tasted like mirepoix, an aromatics stock base, a mixture of onions, celery, and carrots. An interesting attribute of her is that her fingertips always smelled like garlic or onions or whatever scent of what she had recently been chopping, wafting off of her fingertips, and the smell would never wash off. A trait she held in common with my future rebound love, the sous chef, Cesar.

I didn't know all of this then, in fact, she was reticent, and it took me years, decades really, when we were together and also after we were separated to suss and sleuth all of this information out. Because I've learned that relationships, when they are the earth-shattering, major loves of your life breed, will stick on you limitlessly or at minimum stay with you for years, and potentially hauntingly, your entire lifetime.

Curious by her skittishness I asked, "What instrument do you play? And where at, so late?"

She explained, "It's not an instrument at all but my roll of German kitchen knives."

I thought that was a pretty bad-assed thing to carry around on your shoulder for a delicate and petite woman with a lithe swimmer's body. She'd later take me to Broadway Panhandler to shop for proper culinary utensils and supplies. Gifts for my birthday or special occasions would usually involve extravagant meals and *crème brûlée* dishes and a torch or some such endearing and chef-related stuff.

This answer did not fit the caricature I had already created of her persona in my head, and it was frankly the last thing I had expected her to say. She was like that, elegantly shocking and conservatively transgressive, a teasing smart-ass, that dared you to challenge her decorum. She graduated summa come laude from Tufts in anthropology. Classically she speaks innumerable languages and has the demeanor of a wan scholar. She lends a pensive hesitancy and thoughtfulness to every response she gives to any question she's asked. She explained that in her country, unlike the partitioned and strata-driven U.S., everyone, and anyone can be an intellectual.

The butcher, the baker, and the candlestick maker can all belong to the intelligentsia, it's not correlated to how they make their living. Another favorite saying of hers from the university, "Correlation is not causation." This was a snarky quote she threw out when she felt my effusive and overwrought emotions were clouding our arguments or interactions. It was a right and proper verbal smack across the face to shush me into no longer stating an opinion that bristled her buttoned-up emotions. Or simply to silence, when she thought she was correct, there was no arguing otherwise, one of the few ways she revealed her hidden topness. That's the quality that every lover across the gamut, no matter how they outwardly appear to have nothing in common, actually internally do. My recurring theme and motif.

She had the most delicious accent on her English. She would formulate some words and slide them around in her mouth when she spoke. Like she was rolling gelato around with her tongue—the pronunciation so elegant I will never forget some of the audible memory. Pure poesy and music, there was something in her speech patterns and pacing that was unusual but so lovable and endearing. My ex-husband gave a name to it—describing someone that has no physical type but just compelling qualities about someone that sends you into their arms, this may simply be it, but I like to believe there is far more to it than that.

She'd had a school girl speech impediment of stuttering, and I found that so deliciously endearing combined with her fierce intelligence and stalwart opinions. Sometimes it's the simplest and most uncomplicated features of a person, that make you fall and stay madly in love with them. That moment when you look over at them while stirring your espresso while waiting for dessert to be served that you could absolutely spend every waking and living moment with this person because they are so exceptional to you.

When she spoke in English, she was quiet and understated, but when she would call home and speak to her Babbo, in Italian, she'd pace around the apartment wildly gesticulating and emphatically yelling. An entirely different personality when she would jump between languages. It was remarkable and fascinating to behold. It irked her when I inelegantly brought this up. Because she wouldn't just switch languages but entire cultures. She had an Italian passport and an American one—very symbolic of her identity. She wasn't just bisexual, she was biracial and bicultural. A very curious person and that was what was so lovable and endearing about her. She was very reminiscent of the Roman god Janus, with a double face, one in both directions. Just like our love, transitions, changes, doorways, endings and time.

She was a perfect storm of qualities and character-istics. No one like her in all of the world. I know people say this all of the time, especially with one of the few great loves in their life. But part of me will always, always, *always* be in love with her. Whether I'm thinking of her or not. It's been over a decade since we were full-blown and full-time lovers but our experiences will stay with me. And whenever we meet up again, from time-to-time, it's like no time has passed between the last time we were together, like a pause button being released and we are back on.

It's not in a still-holding-a-torch-for-her-way, it's just the reality, admittedly. She usually sends me a crate of prosecco for my birthday, "one bottle for each month of the year." Presumably late, like she is always running. She introduced me to prosecco for the first time in Tribeca, at a little place on a mild

Saturday afternoon we spent tooling around the city together. In Italy, it's served at the beginning of the meal, like a palate opener. Ever since it's sort of always been our thing. And now that I know to add St. Germain's Elderflower liquor to it, I can never turn back, it's my drink of choice for life. Pick your poison and stick with it I suppose. Yet, just as fickle of late, I've been cheating on this self-proclaimed lifelong love with Stella Artois Cidre with Creme de Cassis. But my marriage to it is no less.

The culinary things she taught me far outlasted the length of our relationship. I remember one trip, maybe after she'd already started her emotional affair with the pastry chef, maybe this particular purchase was out of guilt. She would ordinarily and repeatedly buy me tons of extravagant gifts from the airport gift shops. I remember once boldly exclaiming, "This sampler of French perfumes will probably far outlast the time of our relationship." Wistfully, after the partnership dissolved, I would remember this blurted out comment. Every time I would apply this perfume behind my ears until it was used up. It would sting, but the perfumes were beautiful, and the variety of twelve containers suited me because I could mix it up and wear something new every day.

I didn't realize from her submissive, slight, and tentative approach that this was the beginning of our steady but unpronounced courtship. Later in the relationship, I'd buy her a t-shirt in the West Village that read, "I'm not gay, but my girlfriend is." And a keychain that said, "Nobody knows that I'm a lesbian." My wry sense of humor about our tacit closetedness as a couple. Incidentally, this wasn't just for public consumption, this was oddly the way we experienced the interior of the relationship as well. Even her and I in private, we never overtly discussed.

It would vaguely come up when a guy was pursuing one of us and maybe a little bit too persistently. Like when one of her coworkers fell in love with her, and he showed up at our shared apartment to confront me. This would become a recurring theme for us, the crush on her by a coworker. Kitchens are intense environments that I myself have never worked in, but I've loved enough of those who do, to know.

Just like in advertising, intensity breeds emotional attachments. I'm convinced that if the t-shirt did make it as far as the airport in her luggage, out of her perpetual politeness, it ended up in a state-side trash bin after I'd left her at the airport. She thought I was bourgeoisie for any political statements or activism—as something of the past, belonging to the 60's. I always admired her staunch opinions whether agreeable or irrational.

The humor of the t-shirt statement was a play on the fact that we are both bisexual. But a little less on her part. I always joked with her that "You're gayer than all the lesbians in Henrietta Hudson's"—a popular girl bar in the West Village. And also, a rib on the ever closetedness of our affection. But I never hemmed her in with those beliefs either, if she chose me or another woman or later men, her sexual identity and orientation was fluid and ever-changing, like most. We went to dinner with her parents when they came over for a visit while she was still living here and she was visibly alarmed when I'd lean down for something in my purse, and my hair would make physical contact with her person in front of them. Yet she introduced me, in a very formal and traditional way, almost as her fiancé. Her father was a short but handsome man with salt and pepper hair and Santa Clausesque rosy cheeks. He didn't speak a word of English, and interestingly, he would talk to me in full-on Italian, emphatically, while repeatedly pouring me more and more wine to underscore whatever it was he was saying. He was jovial and social if not completely unintelligible to me. It was a ridiculously humorous interaction if I hadn't so dearly wanted to understand what he was saying, and through my association with his daughter, how warmly partial I felt toward him.

As jovial, affable and personable as her father was, she was the arch opposite of cool reserve. Funny. Her uncomfortableness was unspoken like a lot of the things that went on between us as a couple— expressed with a sidelong glance or a tightening of the tension coils of her muscles. I will never forget that introductory meeting at some hipster East Village restaurant her mother had read about in the NY Times Dining Out section, which I used to faithfully collect weekly and bring to her whenever we would travel to Italy.

She always used to say, "We are not gay we are just particularly attracted to one another." I found that comment hollowly in denial but somehow endearingly comforting while confidentially secretive. That was good enough for many years. Although truly statements like that are the seeds of unwaged disputes that wedge between you til there is too much space to bridge—both literally and figuratively in our eventual case.

For example, on a trip to South Beach in Miami we stayed at Hotel Leon, it was a tiny but classy bed and breakfast. We were going through one of our sex-driven vacation phases. She would oddly objectify me as strictly a sexual object during certain periods in our relationship. She would scold, "You are reductive, my dear" her knee-jerk response indicating I'd hit a soft spot. It was just a feeling I would get when we were traveling around playing tourist sometimes. Caught in a random moment in a gift shop at a museum or a writer's house, looking at postcards, or magnets that I collect from every destination I visit. She would look over at me, and her thoughts were leering like a certain look a man will give you when you've barely met, or you're complete strangers, and he's having impure thoughts.

We were at one of these tourist hot spots, I can't recall which, possibly Versace's house or the Holocaust memorial or this one famous author's mansion taking a photograph and I had a passerby took a shot of us, and she would get visibly agitated that we were taking a photo as a couple, as if they could deduce the nature of our relationship in that tiny millisecond of taking our picture, or that they even cared either way. This also happened in the JFK airport, and when she picked me up at the airport in Florence for the first time, in her vest, looking like a noble countryman coming back from the hunt or someone from a Vogue spread with dogs and horses. I probably subconsciously knew we were authentically already doomed in these moments, but ever refusing to take off the rose-tinted glasses.

I'd push my consciences quibbling to the edges and write it off as a self-conscious quirk of having her photo taken. This was self-convincing, and anytime you have to argue or rationalize something too much in a relationship, that is a warning flag that it is an ill fit. These push-aways will eventually become threadbare in the relationship, like a frayed rug that will eventually trip you every time you pass over it.

Woody Allen once humorously said, "Bisexuality immediately doubles your chances for a date on Saturday night." But he forgot to mention or even allude to the complications it can bring to that evening. I'm no anthropologist, but sex is the riches everyone is democratically born with, from dirt floors and no running water to the Park Avenue penthouse and the tippy-top of skyscrapers. The freedom of uninhibited sex—the personal is political—unencumbered by religious, political or social mores, couched in a particular place and time, with some personality and temperamental influence, is a natural born right that only some people take full advantage of.

I like to hover in that sexual equivalent of the airport—that liminal space—of no country or nation—I suppose everyone travels with their ethnic, cultural ideologies but my worldview is imposing unwilling freedom on the world. I think it's unfair and unrealistic for a new lover or relationship to expect your heart and body to be a clean slate.

This is what I've learned through my journey of my sexual anarchy. Everyone has a history, some more varied and sundry, and colorful than others. But it's a building up—like layers of fossilized rock, that established a multi-layered experience we all bring to each new experience.

I love to play with gender roles and stereotypes, in and out of the sack. I adore running the spectrum and gamut of gender and sexual identity. NYC is a gold mine and playground for exploring these differences and gender-bending.

Just take the subway, and you can cruise every specimen of ideology possible. Though I don't embody these qualities myself. I'm not a baby butch or a royal queen myself—I relish and adore it in other people—quite the opposite from homophobia and transphobic. I've learned to love and admire how both genders express and embody their sexuality, the politics, and activation of their personality. In dress, expression, and activity.

I may think love and lust do not conquer all as much as I want them too—love and lust can span all previous boundaries and roadblocks. Like I say, I don't have a 'type' because there are so many types, kinds, and breeds. It's not that I can't pick, like a kid in Dylan's candy shop, it's more like I'm O+ blood type, and I can be a donor for any other blood type—gender or sexual identity. I'm a pleasure monger, but it is more than that too, it is a political and erotic stance.

But back to the golden courtship days. She was a Cancerian crab, and for those of you who don't speak astrology, that means she approaches all things in life obliquely. Sidewinding and sidling up to me. I'm a lovely Libra, the reigning Queen of partnership, and endlessly, blindly weighing the pro's and con's, paralyzingly indecisive with a fiery Sagittarius rising and an earthy and sensuous moon in Taurus. I don't even know if I agree with the tenets of astrology, it seems impossible as it has evolved historically and politically, but it is an awesome metaphor to talk about personality characteristics.

She was a water sign that soaks into any available crevices that you don't know are there till the water freezes into ice and cracks your heart like ice does the sidewalk—splitting it into countless puzzle pieces.

That is how we ended up dissolving eventually, sincerely a good and lifelong love, one of the true and great loves of your life, you never get over. You never end up healing the wounds or scars or forgetting the memories or shored moments—for good or ill.

As expected she side-winded up to me. I'd 'courageously' walk her to her room. Her gender-bending approach even from the start. Me, the uber-femme, being her chivalrous knight in shining armor. Every night she'd noncommittally stand in my room doorway, never entering, chatting with her knives on her shoulder. Formally, politely and ceremoniously like we were making conversation over tea and crumpets as if she was waiting to see someone for an appointment. There was a tentative, waiting it out speed to it. I was of course already in a hovering state of mind with my around-the-clock work and visiting my dying father monthly, so I was 'waiting' for his eventual demise as well.

It was a two-fold waiting that lent a thick looming presence to our light-hearted conversations. Like the air when you primally know it is going to rain or storm without the assistance of technology to tell you something was about to happen. I knew, she knew, and yet that powerful presence of the unspoken said it all, in the meantime we said nothing. Sometimes words only serve to break the spell.

After the appropriate courting period, we took our chats outside the apartment on mini semi-dates. Interestingly, even though she didn't drink, we would frequent the Trinity pub. She came along I suppose not to imbibe but to drink in my presence. The bar itself not far from our apartment—a few short blocks and a couple of long avenues away. Whenever restaurants would send us complimentary pairings for each course, because her name was flagged in the system because of her family, she would give hers to me, to graciously accept and share, because of the two of us I was the only drinker.

So the pub was my suggestion, because at the time I drank black and tans, half-harp and half-Guinness, only sufficiently satisfying when properly poured by an authentically brogue-enhanced off-the-boat Irish bartender, tasting differently at the back of the pub, sitting in pew-like, U-shaped padded benches, far too close for friends next to her elbow, below this amazing painting.

Again, this will happen to me time and time again. The initial attraction and early days of an affair, the clichés of everything being impossibly beautiful and food tasting better and the world looking fantastic when you're in love or at least lust.

Additionally, the place resonated with my fine arts background in oil painting, and lent an old world, historical charm to our dates. She had something anachronistic and out of time about her aura, just like the bar. From snack selection to clothing details she was a throwback. Not as far as Florence in its heyday or the glory of the Roman Empire or Emperor's of China but much more out of time than you'd expect of someone so youthful.

I can still see, like it was this morning, her face break into a smile, like a flower blooming at dawn, the way her nose would get rounder and her lips soften. The Trinity pub had this amazing duotone painting at the back of men imbibing Guinness pints, in the home country. Though the pub was frequented by hip and hipster Upper East Siders, it gave an air of authenticity to the ambiance, regardless.

She was incredibly aloof and physically standoffish, always keeping her distance both emotionally and physically. Like the soft and tender meat inside the hard shell of a crab. I recall night after night of longingly wanting to tenderly and delicately brush the stray hairs off of her face. But when it's girl-on-girl action because homosexual just sounds way too medical, there exists this double-question of are you gay or bi? AND do you like me? Because in a usual mating or pairing, you need to find out if the person likes you or is interested in you "that way," is there an attraction is a huge part of the equation, whether for a sloppy, drunken one-night stand hook-up or a long-term relationship. But in this case, I hung back on my approach, normally much more forward and aggressive about going after who I want, because in the case of closetedness and a girl hitting on an inexperienced or potentially straight girl, it's doubly tricky to make that first move. Not so much out of fear of sexual rejection, but the danger of losing the friendship when you sincerely like the person in more than one way.

There is that moment when your affection for a person, in a same-sex attraction, can go either way, satisfactorily. It's delightfully confusing and stimulating at the same time.

Establishing relationships or at least budding sexual attractions are made of these fleeting moments. We make fate-altering choices on the slightest whimsy of libido and carefree nonsense. I held back on her account, not my own. There was something so endearing about her impossibly clompy fine leather Cesare Paciotti boots on her little stick-like legs. She had two modes of dress—formal, fashionable dressy and uber-casual. She wore practical athletic clothing from Paragon Sports in Union Square that doubled between casual wear and kitchen wear when she was dressed down. Later we'd shop together, the old married couple, she'd later buy me matching boots in Florence and pants that zip off into shorts for my environmental biology studies in the rainforest of Mata-Atlantica, Brazil. The cliché of the old couple, fashioning themselves after one another, and her idiosyncratic style winning the day. Her as the butch and top in the relationship, even if the androgynous one, forging the way, and me the femme and bottom, willingly and obediently following her lead. It's a quirk of my own that I prefer to be dominated in bed, but outside I am a fairly loud and dominating personality and usually attract more silent and moody types that drive—both literally, the car, and figuratively, the relationship.

For fear of exoticizing her, in my teens, when I learned to draw the proportions of the face in anatomy and figure drawing, Eskimo and Native Americans have a different distance between nose, chin, and forehead as well as eye distance. So when I first met her, I presumed she was Eskimo, from her features, her wide but pert nose, her almond-shaped eyes, that when warmed by affection looked like milk chocolate chips melting in a double boiler. Instead, she was part American-Chinese, maternal family from Hawaii, her mother married her father on a college trip to Florence. She was a compendium of the characteristics of the East meets West cultures.

She had pin straight hair that somehow constantly still managed to look tousled and unkempt. Hence my knee-jerk reaction to brush it away, because she was so buttoned up and tightly knotted in every other way imaginable. The rebellious hair, defying gravity in all its straightness. She embodied these counter qualities—the uniqueness that make all of us so especially individual, I suppose. I'm always flabbergasted by all that goes into making a person who and how they are—socioeconomic and educational background— and how they manifest these things.

Randomly, smoothing her hair one late evening at the Trinity pub, I leaned in and simply, sweetly and unaggressively kissed her because my instincts, true always, knew she wanted to but never would, in a million light years. So even as the femme in the lesbian but hetero-based-paradigm, I still had to make the first move. Otherwise, I'd be added to the endless queue of almost-was and the-one-that-got-away relationships she had chronically had, a repeating cycle and pastime her entire life.

Usually someone, a teacher, a friend or otherwise, in love with her from a distance or simply unconsummated. That is part of her dire Catholicism or at least nun-like virginal essence.

The first time we ever spent the night together it was more like a slumber party. She invited me to be her guest at a friend's wedding in Ronkonkoma, NJ. She invited me to stay in her hotel with her, and she ordered me a rollaway cot bed, always the picture of propriety, even though it was her intention to seduce me that night. We stayed up all night talking and chatting in bed. Ever evading exactly where we both knew and agreed at this stage this affair was going. And later, when I'd stay at her hotel in the countryside of Tuscany she'd keep us sleeping in separate rooms, I've no idea how we managed so much sex with all this time spent closeted.

It was tentative at best but as racy as that sounds to a majority of the population because we were both women. It was relatively conservative, not the sex, we may have made out kissing while sitting up a bit that night, but the tenor of the relationship as a whole. She had a nun-like essence and could have worn a habit with as much ease as her athletic-wear. She wore fifties underwear as she called it. Plain white briefs and as close to a training bra as a grown woman could choose. She would call the refrigerator an icebox, another 50's or further, throwback.

A lot of times there is a slight ESL component to communicating with a foreign lover, but with her mother's American citizenship and her attending an ivy league American university, there was less of that than usual. But our language, just like our concept of time, was cultural, and there was endless friction based in these crevices and differences.

One night she had me waiting so long that I locked her out of our apartment and no longer wanted to see her. She had decided to walk home over 160 blocks uptown. She had a slight sweat along the sides of her linen shirt and a misting of sweat on her creamy skin. But she'd just up and decided to walk the impossible distance and not phone after saying she was on her way home.

I reminisced on this argument, when I was waiting for a connecting flight in Rome and the first flight to leave of the day on Al' Italia, and the stewardess at the desk to board the plane was on the phone and getting an espresso and walking back and forth, it was hours on end, and it was inconsequential and unacknowledged, no announcements, no explanations—I'd be lucky if and when the plane got off the ground. Wait for it and appreciate. Somehow that waiting and watching these airline workers futz around unnecessarily made me understand her pace and her concept of time ... that had nothing to do with my own. I loved that difference about her instead of the absolute fury at her hours upon hours of lateness. I completely accommodated her and adjusted myself to her patterns and habits.

She was the epitome of androgynous, and it was so comfortable on her, it hung off of her temperament, like her finely tailored Italian clothing or a cologne scent that so perfectly suits someone you couldn't imagine them freshly showered and without it on. It wasn't even a construct of gender identity or strata of the gay and lesbian community. It was just her and a compendium of the choices made by her strong will and character. She embodied her own identity that was so unique and particular to her, it was like an electrical force.

By American standards, she seemed a push-over in her over-developed politeness and straight-backed propriety. But she was steely underneath her marshmallow exterior. In another era, she'd have been an uptight Englishman in a bowler hat, studying at Oxford or a rich landowner running an estate in South America somewhere. Again, time out of mind, as the saying goes. She always said that "American women, and me in particular, don't realize how seductive they are portraying themselves as because it is ingrained in the culture." She used Brittany Spears as the quintessential example of unwitting American brazen sexuality.

She defies time and place, and that was part of her intoxicating charm. But no heady floral fragrance. She'd be an earthy and woody fragrance, like patchouli, but less clichéd and less reminiscent of a Grateful Dead concert—just natural and authentic.

When we spent time together in any country, vacationing or living together, or traveling back and forth to see each other four times a year when she moved back, I would breathe her in and feel as if I'd spent time in a countryside with lots of trees and foliage, with cleaner lungs and a healthy skip to my step. Entirely rejuvenated, like when you spend time in nature and you end up like a watch that gets its gears finely tuned, and you run a lot better after the adjustment. Her calm is that eternal strong and yet changeable seasons of mother nature.

When she made love to me, it was both earthy guttural and at the same time spiritual and elevated. In the beginning, it started very slowly. We were exploring one another and this new experience. In this way we couldn't have been more opposite, her with her chastity, I'm not sure of any of her past loves, unrequited and near misses, if she'd slept with anyone at all, and me with my basketball player numbers, I'd lived with women on and off for years. But even the first time I ever slept with a woman, when I was nineteen and living with the graduate students, in multiple concurrent polyamorous relationships, I instinctively knew what to do my first time even though I'd never previously crossed the line sexually touching a woman before.

Unlike her, I'd kissed women and made love to them by then, that's how Betty approached me, she went with me to see my favorite band, the Hannibals, I was in unrequited love-lust with the lead singer, and I thought it strange that she was doing a sort of striptease dance to catch his attention in front of the stage, she knew I liked him because my personality is ridiculously effusive when I have a crush on someone. It is hours of entertainment just pining and rehashing their details of look and personality and any meetings or path crossings.

This was my first sign that something was amiss with her, and later Tim, that I wasn't privy too, I didn't realize at the time she was forcibly trying to get my attention, not his. Later I'd find out that she and Tim had already discussed this, that they both liked me, and argued over who could have me, when I went to rent the room. During that evening, she was in the, "I'm ditching my boyfriend to hang with you" mode. Then at the end of the night, she kissed me on the pathway leading up to the house. I remember thinking as our lips were locked, how odd that her live-in boyfriend was probably watching this transpire from their attic bedroom window.

I don't believe Betty had ever been with a woman either, before me, just like Nella, even though she was much my senior at the time, she was a bit of a geeky scientist, shyly pretty hiding behind awful eyeglass frames.

My first official ménage à trois was also my first experience with a woman. Betty was as inexperienced as me, but I sort of instinctively knew what to do, like I'd played this role before. I remember, asking her to straddle my face, since she was too shy and sort of frozen deer in headlights style. We may have been high, in the pot filled smoky haze of their attic where, she a botanist, grew pot. She obeyed my request and grabbing her ass cheeks and bearing down her hips to eat her out. I think I was emboldened by her reticence.

I remembered being surprised by my own request and sudden naturalness with something I'd never done before nor had any clue how or what to do next. Because she didn't have the foggiest, I just sort of took the lead by default, but it was oddly comfortable and familiar for no apparent reason.

Tim was there, but it was more of a sidelines participation. Later he and I would end up in a full-blown relationship for years following the disintegration of their relationship. He was in full on voyeur mode for our initial threesome. But later he would take center stage. Betty always said Tim looked like Tom Cruise. I knew then it was strictly his idea, because a girl that enamored would never have suggested polyamory.

This comment was always accompanied by a girlish giggle, and I knew by the way she admiringly said this that she was madly in love with him and this whole ménage was probably initially his idea and not going to pan out in the end. He was exceedingly good looking, but no Tom Cruise, he was tall and slim. She ended up moving back home when her father passed away, and those two fell off with the distance, and I was still living there, still in the same house, but we oddly kept our original rooms, and another man moved in, and for awhile we had a three-way with Tim, him and I. But that fell off as well, the momentum of the relationship between Tim and me was too strong to allow in an outsider after our initial romp.

Death and others seem to perpetually punctuate my love life. So even when I begin a relationship with a clean slate with both a boy and a girl on equal footing, the bisexual dream, the correlations between the parties involved always change the dynamic. Whether it is the closeness or proximity of the remaining two or a shift from the original two, the permissions and the chemistry and dynamics always alter and change organically.

***

Even with my history, it was all sincerely new and fresh with her, as if I was experiencing this for the first time as well. With true and expansive love it resets the clock as it were, my hundreds of lovers collapse into this one single and solitary love and moment in time.

That may have been the budding of love, and then it transforms and transfixes an experience with someone. She left me for the pastry chef that worked in her kitchen, "Close as two Carabinieri," was the way the news was broken to me.

You know the old adage, better to have loved and lost than never to have loved at all? Yea, well, I beg to differ. It's complete and utter bullshit. So don't even try to fool yourself.

In many years, from the ground zero epicenters of the heartbreak and break up, maybe even decades in some cases, you may get some insight into the relationship and yourself, but I guarantee you that you won't feel any better or less heartbroken. I may forget for a while or get distracted. That's my coping mechanism—distract myself to forget.

What's done is done. And if your heart has cracked ribs and is hung up in traction for a year or multiply that by the magnitude of the love and lust.

Rest assured, it cannot be fixed or healed. It will never look or feel the same as if you have been in a horrific car or motorcycle accident, I guarantee you, it's like someone with a broken bone that heals over, but the finger or nose are always mildly bent up.

I don't know what's worse, the clean break or the slow and painful death of the relationship. I have a friend that says I don't like endings but that's not totally the case, it's that I acknowledge that connections are like education they shouldn't and don't really end or finish. Whether we acknowledge or not. If you're connected to someone so intimately, where your souls, bodies, and spirits have melded together and forged a new metal together, there's no extracting the alloy, there's no way, except to melt down the new metal, possibly risk burning it off and going back to the original state. There's no unlatching the latched. Therein lies the rub. It's both the beauty and the liability.

People will bristle at that statement like I want it to be so, but it's like muscle memory for professional athletes. A path has been established, so it flows that way automatically.

Contributors

Pamela Brodman

Born and raised in Spain, Pamela Brodman is a retired US Air Force veteran who served more than fifteen years, and an English major student at the University of Nebraska Omaha.

Combining her adventurous life experiences with her passion for writing, she creates vivid fictional stories that resonate with readers.

Pamela lives with her spouse and their four dogs, opening up their home to foster dogs from different local rescue groups.

Flo Golod

Flo Golod lives in south Minneapolis with her husband Scott Bartell. Semi-retired, she's active in the Master Gardener Program.

Her stories have appeared in two issues of Talking Stick, one receiving a second-place award, and in the online journals of Manifestations and BoomerLit.com.

Like her characters, her sexual identity s fluid. Over the years, certain themes have emerged. How does one find and keep love, raise children, make a living at something useful and resist the forces of evil without going nuts?

Pam Flores-Lowry

Pam Flores-Lowry was born and fed in Mar del Plata, Argentina. She moved to Virginia to be with the love of her life, a Fauquier County musician.

In her free time, she runs an almost impossible, for her, nine-minute mile every day, and bakes really tasty blueberry muffins.

She has published fiction both online and in print. One of her stories, "Perfection" was published in Kiss & Tell: Aa Temptation Press Anthology.

To read more about her writing journey, please visit https://medium.com/@pamfloreslowry and follow her on Instagram @pammdq.

Pam is currently working on her first novel.

Malorie Mackey

Malorie Mackey is a published author, having previously published the full-length memoir, *My Playboy Story: Hopping from Richmond to Hollywood* in early 2017 (previously published as *Everyone's Best Friend at Playboy* with First Edition Design Publishing in 2016).

Since publishing her first book, she has been hired as a writer with Viva Glam Magazine. She has published many articles for their online magazine including, *To Understand Hef, You Must Understand His History, My Experience at the Rise Lantern Festival, Why Evita's Style is Classic and Timeless, The Top 5 Benefits of Hot Yoga,* and *The Best Fall Hikes in Southern California.*

Valerie Taylor

A twenty-year resident of NYC, originally hailing from Bloomfield Hills, MI via Chicago and Florida, Valerie is currently a member of Columbia Fiction Foundry. She has a BA in Literature from Columbia and an MS in User Experience Design from KSU. Valerie studied literature and has been a fiction writer and avid journaler for thirty years. A designer by trade and adjunct professor of typography, color theory, web development/design and Adobe software at NYU SPS, Parson's | The New School and CUNY | Baruch as well.

Valerie has written three novels, all in the series and volumes vein. Dirty Girl Diary: Misadventures of a Sexual Anarchist, is a collection of intertwined and related short stories, that has many more volumes, as each chapter is oriented by another character, their job and a quote.

Next, is Wayfinding in Love and Beautiful Delusions.

She is currently working on the nascent beginnings of Petty Tyrants, an espionage technology novel, less introspective and chick lit than the other writings, more masculine and entertaining, but also designed as volumes and series.

Ze Luiz

Ze Luiz is an LA-based writer of poetry, short fiction and literary nonfiction. Having grown up in a diverse urban environment, he has always been interested in the people and places around him, and the stories that each of these has to share; those that often go untold.

His work has been featured in Meat for Tea: The Valley Review, Rigorous, Sky Island Journal, Jelly Bucket, OTHER. Magazine, The Scene & Heard Journal, and Authorship by The National Writers Association.

Other Works from Temptation Press

Summer Fling: Tales of Seduction
Kiss & Tell
The Professor
Private Lessons

Coming Soon
from Temptation Press

Her Afternoon

Dreams Can Come True

A Note from the Publisher

How to Thank a Contributor

Dear Reader,

Everyone at Temptation Press would like to thank you for reading *Choices*. If you would like to thank a particular contributor, the best way is to leave a review for them. You may do so by leaving one on our Goodreads page, under the title, *Choices*, by using the link below:

http://www.goodreads.com/TemptationPress

and be sure to mention the contributor directly.

Why leave a review? Reviews help budding authors build their credibility in the book industry. By posting a review on Goodreads, you help other readers find new authors they may wish to follow, and you never know, your review may end up on an author's website one day.

Friend us on Goodreads:
https://www.goodreads.com/TemptationPress

Visit our website:
http://www.TemptationPress.com

www.ingramcontent.com/pod-product-compliance
Lightning Source LLC
Chambersburg PA
CBHW051115050726
47592CB00002B/835